Imperfect

A novel

By

Monique Shantay

ISBN-13: 978-0692117033

ISBN-10: 0692117032

Any references to historical events, real people, or real places are used fictitiously. Names, characters, places are products of the author's imagination.

Front Cover images provided by Creative Commons

Book Design by Monique Shantay

First Printing edition 2018.

www.moniqueshantay.com

In loving memory of

Cleveland Bernard Smiley

July 10, 1965 – July 6, 2017

You will be in my heart forever

Chapter One

My momma used to always say that life was not a fairytale. I never wanted to believe her. From a young age, I was determined to achieve my happily ever after. For a while, I thought I had done just that. I was working towards my dream job of being a singer-songwriter and I found the perfect fairytale love in my boyfriend, Jesse. The brother was fine. He looked as if he were dipped in bronze with dazzling hazel eyes, a cover boy smile, and a body even the gods would pray for. I thought I had everything a girl could want until I came home one fateful April night.

I parked my white Mazda 6 along Lincoln Park West in front of the apartment building where I lived with Jesse. I figured it a possibility he would be tired from working at the firm with his father but I was really in the mood to catch a movie and I hoped he'd be up for it. I walked up the stairs to

1

my third floor apartment and unlocked the door. The living room was dark and still aside from the glow of the television. I placed my purse on the island bar, taking notice of the back of Jesse's head as it leaned over the couch. I would have assumed he was asleep, but his head rocked up and down like a pendulum. I could hear the sound of moaning as I tipped quietly across the carpet to the side of the couch. A woman's head bobbed up and down between Jesse's legs. I could see the bone-straight weave kneeling before him as a soundtrack of pleasure played in the home where I laid my head. I was the uninvited witness to their symphony. As I stood in shock trying to figure out if I wanted to cry or cause bodily harm, Jesse's eyes focused on me. The look on his face switched from pleasure to sheer horror. He shoved the unknown woman from his manhood and jumped to his feet with his pants around his ankles. She stumbled, crashing into the coffee table as I flipped the light switch, shedding light on their illicit act.

"Kamila…" he stuttered.

"That's right," I said, forcing my voice through the betrayed lump that formed in my throat as angry tears burned my cheeks.

"I can explain."

"Explain what?"

The unknown woman fixed her floral pink blouse and stood to her feet while adjusting the weave that brushed past her waist. She looked at me as if she didn't know whether to apologize, introduce herself, or run for her life.

"Let me help you out," I snarled at her with clutched fists as my body shook with anger. "You can finish what you're doing. Obviously, I should knock before entering my own home." I spun on my heels, walking towards the front door.

"Kamila…" Jesse continued to stutter. "Baby, wait."

I turned back to him with all the rage I could muster.

"Oh, now I'm Baby?" I shouted. "Now?"

"Kamila, calm down. The neighbors…"

"Do NOT tell me to calm down," I screamed. "You do not get to tell me to calm down. Fuck these neighbors and fuck you!"

I stormed towards the hall closet next to the front door and pulled out Jesse's Louisville Slugger. The woman's eyes widened.

"This really has nothing to do with me," she whimpered, reaching for her purse. "I'll let you two be alone." She pushed Jesse towards me and ran to the door, attempting to leave. I step backward and cut her off by shoving her into the wall.

"Oh no, this has EVERYTHING to do with you," I hissed. "Like I said, go back and finish what you started."

"Kamila, will you stop it and talk to me?" Jesse cried.

"Now you want to talk?" I swung the bat in my hand as I stepped towards the end table in the living room. On the end table sat an antique floral lamp that was given to us by Jesse's mother. I swung the bat back and forth and lifted it over my head, bringing it down with the full force of my hurt onto the lamp. Pieces of glass flew across the room. Jesse and the woman shielded their faces, trying not to get cut.

"Kamila, stop it!"

"Fuck you, Jesse! You'd better be lucky that it wasn't your head!" I swung open the door and ran out of the apartment, down the stairs, still holding the baseball bat. Jesse adjusted his clothing and followed behind me.

"Kamila!" he called. I turned to watch as his slut bunny ran barefoot in the opposite direction of the street, carrying stilettos in her hands.

"Would you stop? You're making a scene!"

"You're lucky it's not a fucking crime scene," I snapped. "Get away from me, Jesse!" I stormed towards my car but Jesse jumped in between me and the driver side door. He stared at me as his eyes began to water. I stared back with pure anger.

"Move!" I shouted.

"Not until you talk to me," he commanded, grabbing my wrist. "You need to come upstairs and stop acting crazy."

"Why would I go anywhere with you?"

"Because you belong with me," he responded. I tried to pull my wrist away from him, which only caused him to tighten his grip. "Come upstairs."

"Let me go, Jesse! You're hurting my wrist!"

We continued arguing as flashes of red and blue light began to hover over us. Jesse looked around and released his grip, looking at me with resentment. After all, Jesse was a Bennett and Bennetts had images to maintain. He mouthed to me.

"See what you did?"

"You and your slut did this," I whispered. We looked on as a CPD squad car parked behind my car. A young man with blond hair, appearing to be no more than 25 stepped from the car, walking toward us.

"Hey, hey!" he shouted. "What's going on? I received a call about a noise disturbance."

Jesse stared at me, looking as if he was annoyed at my insistence on being angry with his infidelity and inconveniencing his life.

"Officer," Jesse explained. "I'm simply trying to have a discussion with my girlfriend." As much as I wanted to respond in anger, this was 2018. Black bodies were being spilled on the streets at the hands of police and I was not trying to be one of those black bodies. I took a deep breath, trying to pull all of the private school education I could from my being.

"I apologize for the noise, officer," I said, trying to remain calm. "I didn't mean to disturb the neighbors. I simply had a disagreement with my boyfriend and I'd just like to go home now." The police officer gave Jesse a curious look before returning his focus to me.

"Why are you holding a bat, ma'am?" the officer asked. *Oh shit, I'm going to jail*, I thought to myself.

"It belongs to my younger brother," I lied. I trembled with nervousness as I looked at Jesse, my eyes begging him to go along with my lie. I was always a horrible liar.

"Yes, I borrowed it for my company's baseball game. I work at the Law Offices of Bennett and Howard. My father is Gerald Bennett." He reached into his wallet and pulled out his business card. He was an excellent liar. It was at that moment I was sure he'd have a very promising career practicing law.

The young officer's hardened exterior softened as he examined Jesse's business card. He looked and smiled at Jesse, passing the card back to him.

"Oh yes," the officer replied. "I'm familiar with your father. You two just keep it down. You know there are lots of older people around here who don't like to hear all of that ruckus."

"Of course," Jesse responded, flashing a convincing smile. The officer returned to his car and sat for a moment before driving away. Jesse took a relieving sigh as his poker face melted away, returning to his previous look of anger and desperation.

"Now can we please talk?" he begged.

"You've already displayed your expert lying skills tonight, Jesse. You don't need to do it anymore." I shoved past him and got in my car. He stepped back, holding up his hands in defeat. I assumed he didn't want to cause any more of a scene.

***

I drove across town to the three flat building my family owned on the south side of town. I walked up the stairs to my mother's apartment on the second floor where she sat in the living room with my uncle, Silas, watching an episode of *Supernatural.*

"Hey Ma," I said. "I'm gonna stay downstairs at Big Momma's apartment for a while." Momma flashed me a frustrated look as she paused her DVR player.

Momma's voice was a dry as sandpaper as she asked, "What happened? What did you do now?"

"I don't want to talk about it. I just need to stay downstairs for a while and wanted to let you know." She stood to her feet, straightening her curly, sandy blond wig as she faced me. The smell of vodka poured from the pores of her petite, 5'1 frame.

"So you're just letting me know?" she asked with a sarcastic smile. "Do you think this is a Motel 6 and you can come and go as you please? What did you do to Jesse?"

I began to lose awareness of the exhaustion in my body as I burned with a simmering anger. I pulled my shoulders back, staring into the cold brown eyes of the woman who brought me into the world. Silas looked on, taking notice of the tension in both of our faces. Standing at 6'4 and weighing about 350 pounds, I watched in amazement as my uncle jumped over the coffee table with an agility that reminded me of my childhood cat, Rocky.

"Sheila, stop it," he intervened. "You know Momma left this building to all three of us. Nobody's down there. If she needs to stay in Momma's place, let her." My mother and I continued exchanging angry stares at each other as Silas looked back and forth between the two of us, longing for some form of peace.

"I'm too tired for this," I said through gritted teeth. "I'm going to bed." I turned towards the door as my mother's words shot burning arrows towards the back of my head.

"She blew it with Jesse just like she blew it with school." I paused.

"Just like you blew it in school?" I retorted, before slamming the door behind me.

Chapter Two

I felt as if anvils were tied to my arms, legs, and emotions, pulling me with heavy force as I laid in my grandmother's bed. Rays of sun beamed through the sea-green curtains as I shut my eyes, rejecting the coming day. However, my attempts to hide away in dreamland were for naught as I was disturbed by loud bangs on the bedroom door. I sat up on my grandmother's bed with a huff, wiping the saliva from the side of my face.

"Wake up, bitch!" Dionne called from the other side of the door.

"Go away," I moaned.

"Bitch, you'd better not be naked because I'm coming in!" My best friend pushed the door open and stepped inside. She pursed her prominent motherland lips at me as she entered with heavy steps that boomed across the creaky wooden floor. She commanded me, "Get your ass up!"

"How'd you know I was here?" I groaned.

"Your momma," she said, placing one hand on her hip, appalled that I would dare question the powers of a gossiping mother. "Now get your ass out of that bed and tell me what happened."

I hunched my shoulders and with a heavy breath, I explained, "He cheated on me,"

"Oh no," Dionne plopped down on the bed next to me, wearing a shocked expression as she gave my shoulder a comforting rub. "What happened?"

"Oh not much. I simply walked into my own home to discover some possibly disease-ridden tramp with her head in his lap." The tears resumed, stinging my exhausted face as Dionne wrapped her arms around me.

"Oh no," she whispered. "Don't cry. I can kill him if you want."

"No," My mouth quivered, struggling to continue on its train of blubbering.

"I can do it. I'm the daughter of a killer. It's in my blood." My mouth fell from its blubber train, responding with a faint laugh.

"That's my bitch," Dionne laughed. "Now let's work on some music!"

"Ugh, I can't right now," I protested. "I'm too drained. Plus when I came back here, I got into a fight with Sheila."

"Oh, y'all fight all the time. Use it!" Dionne was filled with excitement as she jumped from the bed, running into the dining room to Big Momma's stereo system. She took a CD from her tan shoulder bag and placed it into the CD player. An instrumental with a vintage New York sound roared throughout the dining room as Dionne opened the pink curtains, welcoming the sunlight.

"I can't write to this one," I whined, dragging myself out of bed into the dining room. I took a seat at the large mahogany table, digesting the music that my prolific producer friend created. "Not right now. This one deserves some profound lyrics. All I have in me right now are anger and tears."

"That's fine," she smiled as she changed the track. The trippy sound of a more melancholy beat graced my ears. I closed my eyes, watching colors and words swirl around in my mind. Lyrics began to form as I reached for my purse that hung on the adjacent chair. I pulled my notebook and pen from the purse and began to scribble.

I can't believe it/ My heart lays in tiny pieces

I normally don't show weakness/ But here I sit defeated

The words continued to pour from me. Some of them made sense. Others, not so much. But I poured all of my pain onto the paper as Dionne looked on with eagerness.

Dionne and I had been friends since we were kids, growing up together in the Cabrini Green housing projects on the north side of Chicago. We immediately connected as sisters, which was refreshing to both of us considering neither of us had actual siblings growing up. Although our mothers were never very close, Big Momma made sure that Dionne and I stayed in touch once our families fell victim to gentrification in the late nineties. Dionne and her mother moved to the west side while we moved south. Big Momma would take two busses to get Dionne for sleepovers whenever we would want to hang out. During one of our sleepovers, Dionne snuck and read my notebook. I was furious when I found out and we didn't speak for a week, but once we reconnected, she encouraged me to start writing songs. Initially, we would just perform around the house or around the neighborhood but she met a friend in college who taught her how to produce music. After that, we took a more serious interest in music, performing as a group at talent shows and open mics around town. I loved performing with Dionne so much that I left DePaul University where I was working towards an accounting degree. As good as I was with math, I found the field to be an unnecessary level of boring. I only pursued that career path to please Big Momma and I was quite sure that if she were still alive, she would have put me in the dirt for walking away. Accounting still paid the bills during the day but at night, I was a singer-songwriter.

While I was in my creative zone, the music was joined by the sound of a closing door, followed by footsteps. I looked up to see my mother standing in the doorway wearing a disapproving look on her face.

"Still trying to be Missy Elliot?" she asked with a slight roll of the eyes. I gave her a blank, silent stare as she stepped further into the room. "Is this why you threw away your college degree?"

"I'm not trying to fight with you today, Mother," I sighed.

"I'm not here to fight. I'm fixing lunch and I need you to go to the store."

"Why do you need me to go?"

"Because I already started on lunch and I forgot a few things. Come on, Kamila."

"Okay," I responded. "Give me the money." She placed a twenty dollar bill on the table in front of me.

"I need some sugar, nutmeg, and bell peppers."

"Gotcha." I took the money from the table. My mother and I had always had a strange relationship. She became pregnant with me at the age of sixteen, giving birth when she was seventeen. While she was a junior in high school, her high school sweetheart, my father, was murdered. He was one of the many casualties of gang violence that took place in Cabrini Green during the 90s. Big Momma took on the role of being my mother so Momma could finish high school, only she ended up dropping out anyway to run the streets. Throughout my childhood, my mother was either out in the streets, drinking, or just flat out angry with my existence. Much of our days together would be spent at each other's throats and as angry as I would be with her, Big Momma would always be there to gently remind me that she was still my mother whether she acted like it or not. When Big Momma passed away, Silas took on the role as the voice of reason. With their guidance and insistence, I'd always find myself being the bigger person and apologizing to her even when she would be dead wrong. Coming down to ask me to go to the store was my mother's way of ending the argument and returning our relationship from episode of *Jerry Springer* level dysfunction to episode of *Roseanne* level dysfunction.

Taking Momma's money, Dionne and I walked out of the house and down 59th street towards Kedzie.

"Why aren't we driving?" Dionne whined.

"Because I have frustration to burn and you have calories to burn."

"Bitch, are you calling me fat?"

"No," I laughed. "Your inner thighs are calling you fat."

"Hoe, your dun lap has been screaming to you for the past year or so. You know, belly dun lapped over your belt?"

"Real original." The two of us laughed as we continued our stroll down 59th Street. As we crossed Francisco Street, we heard a woman's voice call to us.

"Hey y'all!" We turned and watched as a thin, coffee-colored woman ran through traffic across the street towards Dionne and me. I rolled my eyes as I recognized the girl I loved to hate.

"Hey," Dionne muttered to Janette as she rolled her eyes. I pursed my lips as I looked at Janette. She didn't deserve my words.

"I saw your car last night, Kamila," Janette said. "Trouble with your lawyer friend?"

"He's not my friend, Janette," I responded. "In fact, neither are you. So there's no need for us to continue this conversation." Janette flashed a devilish grin across her thin, burgundy painted lips as she whipped her wet and wavy weave from her shoulders. I was sure she found the weave at the bottom of the clearance box at Dollar Tree, but that was none of my business.

"Now Mimi," Janette replied. "I know you're not still carrying a grudge since I took your man back in high school, are you?"

"Took my man?" My laughter contained sarcasm with a tinge of bitterness as I took a step backward. "If he was low enough to roll around and get fleas with you, he was never my man to begin with. Let's go, Dionne."

"Gladly," Dionne added as the two of us continued on our journey. Janette kept a close distance as she followed behind us.

"You know," she continued. "Y'all always thought y'all were so much better than me because y'all went to college and y'all live these fancy lives. But women like you will always lose men to women like me. It doesn't matter if he's a high school sweetheart or a big-time lawyer. It always happens."

I spun around as anger began to simmer within me. Back in high school, my boyfriend, Demarcus did cheat on me with Janette, who was the neighborhood tramp. Considering what I had gone through the night before with Jesse, Janette was the representation of herself, Demarcus, the mystery slut and Jesse and it was time for someone to pay. Dionne grabbed my arm, noticing the infuriating shade of crimson that had become my face.

"She is not worth it," Dionne whispered. Janette looked at me and laughed.

"Not so high and mighty now," she smirked as she turned to walk away.

***

When Dionne and I made it back from the store, I noticed Jesse's silver BMW parked behind my Mazda. I paused as my body became flooded with anxiety. Dionne studied the car and looked back at me.

"Girl, I told you I could cut his ass," she said. A weighed breath escaped from me.

"No," I responded. "I should have known he'd show up. Let's just get this over with.

We entered the building and walked up to my mother's apartment. 80s house music blared on the radio as we made our way through the front door and dining room to the kitchen where Momma stood by the stove. Jesse sat at the round green kitchen table, appearing to be deep in conversation with Momma.

"What are you doing here?" I snapped at him.

"I invited him," Momma retorted before Jesse could say a word.

"And why would you do that?" I asked.

"You invited yourself, so I invited him."

"Ma, in case you forgot, Grandma left this building to all of us. If I want to come home, I can come home. Now, why is he here?" She released an annoyed grunt, walking away from the stove towards Dionne and me.

"So he cheated. Kamila, stuff happens. Life is not just black and white. There are many shades of gray in between. Hear the man out." She turned her gaze from me to Dionne. "Come on, Dianna and let's go watch some TV."

"It's Dionne, girl. You ain't that drunk yet!" Dionne and Momma left the kitchen, leaving me alone to talk with Jesse. He looked up at me from his seat. The whites of his eyes appeared as if they were dyed a harsh shade of scarlet. The bags under his eyes had bags under their eyes.

"Kamila," he began. "Please hear me out." I circled around him, taking a seat in the chair across from him. He reached out his hand to mine. I pulled my hand away, letting him know without a word that he had not regained permission to touch me just yet.

"Speak," I nodded, giving him a cold stare.

"I'm so sorry," he continued. "It should have never happened, especially not in the home we share together."

"You're right," I responded. "The proper protocol for being a cheating scumbag is to rent a motel to get head from your whores."

"I guess I deserve that. I don't want to fight anymore, Kamila. Cassandra is Hannah's roommate and she was over for a visit. We were drinking and..."

"Why was she in our apartment with you?" I interrupted. "Why were the two of you drinking alone?" I wasn't too surprised to learn his sister had something to do with it. That little pain in the ass never cared for me.

"We weren't alone at first," he responded. "Cassandra came into town from New York and Hannah brought her to the apartment. We were all drinking but Hannah had to leave. Things kind of got out of hand from there. I'm not making excuses for my behavior. What I did was horrible. I'm just asking you to please not throw away three years of our lives together because I made a mistake."

"Great closing argument, counselor," I sniped.

"Kamila, stop it. I'm serious."

"I need time to think," I said. Getting up from the chair, I walked out into the living room where Dionne and my mother sat on the couch. The two of them watched in amusement as some poor girl on *Maury* made her sixth appearance on the show, searching for her baby's father.

My voice burned with intense anger as I asked, "Why did you invite him?"

"You're really going to let that man walk out of your life because he was being a man? I'm trying to keep you from being stupid." Frustration covered me like a blanket as I stared at my mother, thinking of all the responses I could have had for the statements she just made. I thought to myself, *did I really want to spend my days arguing with this woman?* I felt in my gut there was only one thing to do.

"Jesse!" I called to the kitchen.

"Yes, Babe?" he answered, running to my side as if he was expecting some sort of treat.

"I forgive you. Let's go home."

"Of course," he gave a weak smile as he walked towards the front door.

"Aw, y'all leaving?" Dionne whined. "Let me give my brother a hug!" She jumped up from the couch and rushed over to Jesse, wrapping her arms around his neck. With her right hand, she pushed his ear towards her mouth.

"If you hurt my sister again, I will kill you," she said in a loud whisper. His eyes grew wide as his mouth formed into an uncomfortable grin. He pulled her arms away from him.

Chapter Three

Many would say that a Chicago spring actually experiences all four seasons at one time. Although it was late April, it felt as humid as if it were mid-July as I parked my car in front of Dionne's apartment building the next afternoon. Young men who wore the wisdom of hard street lives stood in front of the brown brick building while children walked along the sidewalk, speaking on various grown-up topics. Big Momma probably would have slapped the soul from my body if I was ever fool enough to allow an adult to hear me talking about things like smoking weed and having sex. As I took careful steps over the broken beer bottles towards the building, my body tensed and my breaths became labored.

"What's up, Lil Momma?" one of the men called to me as he sat on the front steps. His friends seemed to examine

me as he stood to his feet, licking his lips as if he was
preparing to devour his prey.

"Hi," I said, folding my arms over my chest. As he
walked around me, I could feel his eyes going over my body as
if they were two overly eager TSA agents.

"So what's your name?"

"Trina," I lied. I never told strange men my real name.

"So when are you gonna come see me?" *See you? Dude,
I don't even know you*, I thought to myself. But I couldn't say that
out loud. I couldn't say anything. I looked around at the men
surrounding me. One of them looked on with concern in his
eyes, which was a welcomed change from the hyena from *Lion
King* vibes the other men seemed to give. That man spoke up.

"Twan, leave that girl alone. She didn't come to see
your ugly ass." Twan's other friends removed their attention
from me as they roared with laughter at their embarrassed
friend. Twan stepped from in front of me, tending to his
bruised ego. The other friends gave him playful shoves,
laughing as I continued on to Dionne's apartment. I did a
quick turn, nodding to thank Twan's friend for saving me
from his advances. I could have shut Twan down myself, but
as he was hitting on me in front of his boys, many things
could have happened and many of those things were not
good. In the past, I had men call me a bitch or a whore

because I wouldn't give them my phone number. One man physically attacked me because in his words, I thought I was all that. A friend who grew up with Dionne and me was stalked and murdered by a man because she thwarted his advances. Twan's friend was a Good Samaritan and chances were he might have saved my life.

I entered the building and knocked on the door to Dionne's first-floor apartment.

"Open the door, Bitch!" I teased.

"I'll open it when I'm good and goddamn ready!" she called from the other side. Dionne's soft frame stood in the doorway dressed in fluffy lavender slippers, lavender boy shorts, and a white tank top. Her bra-length natural hair was pulled into a high pineapple which peaked out of her perfectly wrapped head scarf.

The scent of sage danced through the air as Erykah Badu's *Certainly* played on the stereo system in the living room. Dionne took a seat on the plush lavender rug, pressing her back onto the white leather sofa. She reached for the coffee table to grab the blunt that simmered, waiting for her return.

"You're in here zoned out," I laughed as I sat beside her on the couch.

"I have to be," she responded. "Girl, this here is what keeps me out of prison."

"How does doing something that's clearly illegal keep you out of prison?" I asked.

"Girl, easy," she took a hit from the blunt, laying her head back towards the couch as she looked up at me. "Understand something. This right here keeps me from wanting to slap the hell out of people. I call it my calm-down medicine. Plus it helps me get in the zone so I can be my best female version of Pharrell Williams. I'd say Dr. Dre, but I don't associate with the likes of a misogynistic woman beater."

"I know that's right."

"You need to try some of this one day," she smiled. "You'd enjoy it. Maybe it will calm your angry ass down."

"I am not angry," I replied. "I'm just observant of the fuckery that is the human condition and point it out to the world with an eloquence of a well-educated sailor." We laughed.

"Besides," I continued. "You know Jesse doesn't like that stuff."

"Jesse?" she leaned forward and turned to me, flashing a sarcastic smirk. "How is Mr. Sloppy Toppy?"

"He's okay, girl. You know I moved back home because as many problems as we have, they're nothing compared to dealing with Sheila Winter every day. I love that woman but sometimes I want a DNA test. I don't think she's my mother at all."

"Girl," Dionne laughed. "You're her twin. You know that's your mother." She took another hit of the blunt and exhaled like a seasoned professional as she shook her head at me.

"Yes, maybe so. But that woman is crazy. She's nothing like Big Momma. Things haven't been the same since she's been gone. I really miss her. She'd know what to do if she were here."

"You act like you can't still talk to her," Dionne responded.

"I know I can but it's not the same. My mom just wants me to work things out with Jesse because he has money. You know I'm not that girl. I didn't get with Jesse for his money, contrary to what his family may think."

"So why did you go back?" Dionne asked. "I would have stabbed his ass."

"I went back because we've been together for three years. We've built a life together, although we haven't exactly made it official. As angry as I am at Jesse, I know this isn't the same situation as when Demarcus slept with that human sperm clinic, Janette. I want to believe that this was a onetime thing."

"Maybe it is," Dionne sighed as she straightened her position on the floor. "Look, Kamila. I'm not your big momma. I'm just your homegirl but you know I tell you the real. And the real is only you can decide if you want to stay with Jesse or not. You know I'm down to poke him with an ice pick if you want me to, but if you still want to make him my brother-in-law, I'll support you."

"Thanks, girl," I smiled. Dionne always knew what to say to me.

"Now," she said, finishing her blunt and putting it out in her ashtray. "Can we get down to business?"

"What's up?"

"You know about Exodus over there on the east side?" she asked, joining me on the couch.

"Yeah," I responded. "Over there around 79th and Yates. What about it?"

"They have open mic night on Thursday nights," Dionne's eyes widened as she spoke. "Kamila, I think we should do it."

"I'm down," I shrugged. "I've been writing."

"Cool. Also, are you busy Saturday?"

"Not sure," I responded. "Why do you ask?"

"I was wondering if you could drive with me to the prison to visit my pops."

"You mean downstate?"

"Come on, girl!" she pleaded. "You know I can't drive and even if I could, I don't want to go down there alone. It's been a while since I've seen him and I told him I'd come down for his next visiting day."

"Okay, okay," I relented. "You know I spoil your fat ass."

"Bitch, I know you didn't!"

***

After spending another hour at Dionne's place, it was still a bit early in the day. I was avoiding Jesse so I decided not to go home. After giving a sigh of relief that Twan and his boys were gone from the front stoop, I hopped in the car and turned on Pandora. The Internet's *Get Away* played through my speakers as I took the streets to the family building to spend time with my uncle Silas. It was Tuesday, so I was sure that he was propped on the couch watching *WWE SmackDown*.

I drove straight down Kedzie for what seemed to be forever. By the time I made it to the house, it was after 8. As I arrived, I looked around at the cars parked on Talman Street. I felt relieved as I didn't see my mother's black Dodge Intrepid. *Could it be that she wasn't home,* I hoped to myself.

I walked up to the third floor and knocked on the door to my uncle's apartment. I felt a vibrating sensation coming from my jean pocket and ignored it, sure to myself that the cause of the sensation was a call from Jesse that I was not ready to accept.

"Come in," Silas called from the other side of the door.

As I stepped inside, I was welcomed by the strong scent of Newport cigarettes. Silas sat in his boxers on the center of the burgundy sofa inside his living room which was only lit by his television. He was watching a match between Kevin Owens and AJ Styles as he paused, looking up at me with a smile peeking through his salt-and-pepper goatee.

"Hey, Baby Girl," he smiled. "Came to watch wrestling with your favorite uncle?"

"I sure did," I grinned, running and plopping down on the couch next to him. He lifted his arm and put it around my shoulder as I leaned into his embrace. Suddenly, I felt like that eight-year-old girl he taught how to fight many moons ago after Malcolm and Martin, or as we called them, the dirty twins, pushed me down one day while I was playing at the playground. Momma and Big Momma didn't condone fighting. They said it wasn't ladylike but Silas said that he wasn't going to allow his baby niece to be pushed around by no scrub ass little boys. No matter what went on in my life, I always felt happy and safe around my uncle Silas.

"So where's Ma?" I asked.

"Where you think? Out at the bar with her friends. How have you been?"

"I've been okay," I sighed. His eyebrows furrowed, signaling to me that they were calling bullshit on my lies. "Well… I have been avoiding Jesse."

"I can see that," he smiled. "I mean, I always welcome a visit from my favorite niece but I know you, Lil' Girl. Don't forget I used to change your diapers."

"I know," I sighed. "It's just everything has been so perfect. Why did he have to go and do this?" Every sense of control I had in my body melted away as tears escaped from my eyes, running down my face to freedom. Silas took his rough mechanic's hands and wiped the tears from my face with the softness of a baby's blanket.

"Baby, life isn't perfect," he said. "Now I don't always agree with the things your mama says and does but she was right about one thing. There are lots of shades of gray when it comes to life. When you love someone, they're going to do

31

things to hurt you and you're going to do things to hurt them."

"I won't do anything like that," I protested, sitting up from my uncle's embrace. He shrugged.

"You don't know what you could be capable of in a moment of human weakness. None of us do."

I sank back into the couch and thought over my uncle's words. The cell phone continued to buzz in my pocket.

"I guess what you're saying makes sense," I sighed.

"I know. It always does," he said with a confident smile. "I'm always right." Of course, I knew there was no way Silas could always be right, but he always spoke with a level of confidence and wisdom that could rival the wisest of sages. In my 27 years of life, I don't think I've ever seen the man raise his voice.

Hours had passed as the sunlight peeked through Silas's closed blinds. I opened my eyes to find myself stretched out on the burgundy couch, wrapped in a blue plaid blanket. The smell of pancakes, eggs, and bacon tickled my nose as Silas fixed breakfast in the kitchen. Not only was he wise, but Silas was an amazing cook. I could honestly say he was a better cook than Big Momma.

I got up from the couch and walked through the dining room to the kitchen where my plate was already fixed and calling my name from the blue glass table. Silas poured a glass of orange juice and placed it on the table next to my plate as I sat down to eat.

"Good morning," he smiled. "You seemed tired."

"I was," I grinned. "Thank you for breakfast." I looked up at the pale blue clock on the kitchen wall. 6:25 am. Thankfully, I had plenty of time to eat breakfast with Silas and get to work. I left some changes of clothes in Big Momma's apartment so I could get dressed there.

"Have you had time to think about what you're going to do with this Jesse problem?" he asked.

"I'm going to go home tonight," I replied. "I just needed time without having to deal with him and Momma."

"Your momma means well," Silas said.

"No, she doesn't."

"She does. She just doesn't know how to show it." Silas and I finished breakfast together and I suggested he watch the news while I cleaned the kitchen. Yes, Silas was an amazing cook, but he wasn't the cleanest person and I was sure those dishes would have sat until I came back to visit unless Sheila just happened to be in a good mood one day.

After cleaning the kitchen, I went downstairs to change and pulled my cell phone from my pocket to check my missed calls. There were twelve of them and all but one were from Jesse. I played his final message.

Jesse: Look... I don't know where you are or if you're safe. You could at least let me know that much, Kamila. I understand that you may not want to talk right now. But please come home tonight. At least call me back.

Chapter Four

After work, I decided to go back to my apartment. My heart grew heavy as I noticed Jesse's silver BMW parked out front. As I opened the door to my second-floor apartment, I was greeted by Jesse who sat at the island bar with a glass of brandy in his hand. The soft sounds of Coltrane played across the dimly lit room, setting the depressing scene as if it was part of a Spike Lee Joint.

"I'm glad you came home," he said before taking a sip of his drink.

"Well," I responded. "We had to talk eventually."

"Kamila," he said, standing from the barstool. "Please tell me that we can be saved. I love you. I promise it will never happen again."

"I don't know that," I said with a tone as dry as summer air in Phoenix.

"Kamila…"

"I'm not done, Jesse," I interrupted. "I've heard everything you've had to say. Now it's my turn."

"Please," he said with a polite nod.

"I don't know that it won't happen again. Neither do you. I'm sure that neither of us looked into the future to find us standing here discussing your dick in another woman's mouth."

"You don't need to be crude, Kamila," Wrinkles formed around his nose as he protested.

"Jesse, you physically had another woman's mouth on your penis. Please don't preach to me about ladylike speech right now. You're not in the position to do that."

Jesse growled so loud, I was sure all the neighbors heard. He hated when I cursed or used any sort of graphic language. This was simply not the Bennett way of doing things but I was not a Bennett. I was a Winter. And Winters had our own way of doing things.

"Okay," Jesse relented. "Let's not fight. I don't want to do that anymore."

36

"You don't get it, Jesse. I'm here. I'm home. And I'm even willing to give us another chance. But please don't make the mistake of thinking things will ever be the same again."

"I'm sure it will take some time to get back to normal."

"If we can get back to normal."

"Kamila, I believe we can make it through this if you give it a chance. You know that I want you to be Mrs. Jesse Bennett one day." I tilted my head back, releasing a loud, sarcastic laugh.

"Do you honestly believe we're going to talk about marriage right now? I have one foot out the door and you want to talk about marriage. Should I start squealing and picking out china patterns, Jesse?"

"I don't mean right now, Kamila." His hazel eyes looked as if they had tiny white flags within the flecks of light. I studied him as I breathed with sympathy. I was angry, but even in my anger, I couldn't deny that I missed my tall cup of hazelnut coffee. This man had my heart and one indiscretion would not take away the love I had for him. I moved with heavy steps towards him, pressing my body against his into a tight embrace. I pressed my breasts firmly into his rib cage and sighed, feeling as if I wanted to collapse into him. He gently cupped my chin and lifted my face up to his, pressing his soft lips into mine. He gave me passionate kisses as I parted my lips to welcome his eager tongue. I sighed and moaned as he gripped me tighter, holding me as he stood up from the barstool. I wrapped my legs around his waist as our tongues continued their sweet dance inside our mouths. He moaned, which caused me to moan. He knew I loved the sounds he would make. The pink lace panties underneath my navy jumpsuit began to moisten as he removed his lips from mine, whispering in my ear as he carried me to the bedroom.

"Mm… I've missed you," he whispered.

"Oooh…" I responded through breaths of wanting. "Tell me how much."

"With every fiber of my being." I don't know how he made it from the kitchen through the hallway to our bedroom without missing a beat because I was sure he wasn't watching where he was going. I was even surer I didn't care.

We entered the bedroom and he placed me on the floor. I slid out of my jumpsuit and stood before him in my matching pink bra and panty set. He undressed and pulled out a condom from the nightstand. He pulled down my panties with fervent desire. Shoving me onto the bed and spreading my legs, he kneeled before me as he licked his lips before placing his face between my thighs. I raised my legs and grabbed the back of his head, pushing him deeper as he teased my promised land with his tongue.

"Mm Jesse," I moaned.

"Do you like it, Baby?" he asked between licks.

"Yes, Baby. I love it." I lifted my legs higher as I rubbed myself back and forth on his face.

"I missed you," he whispered.

"I missed you too."

"Don't leave me again."

"Don't leave me." My legs shook as my skin became hot to the touch. I felt electricity shoot through my being as I climaxed onto his tongue and down his chin. He looked up at me, licking his lips. With a devilish grin, he flipped me onto my stomach, shoving his thick, throbbing manhood into me. I arched my back and leaned into his thrusts as he pumped his unspoken apologizes while I screamed and moaned all of the emotions I couldn't release through words. He smacked my ass and demanded that I say his name.

"Jesse!" I cried, reveling in the delicious sting on my backside.

"Say it again."

"Jesse!"

I must have climaxed three times before his thrusts came harder and faster. I looked back as his face shifted from passion to euphoria while he pumped and groaned, making his grand finale. Then he slowed, leaning over to kiss my forehead.

"I love you," he whispered.

"I love you too," I replied as the last remaining bit of energy flooded from me onto the dark green sheets. I lay in bed and looked at this man who owned my heart. The heart that he broke was now flooding with wanting for him. Thoughts began to flood my mind. Maybe we could survive our hardships. Maybe we could be okay. Maybe I would be Mrs. Bennett after all. Maybe…

I opened my eyes two hours later and looked around the bedroom. The room was dark and I could hear faint sounds of Chopin's *No. 1 Nocturne in B-Flat Minor*. I slipped into my white lace nightgown and tiptoed into the living room. Jesse sat at the computer doing what appeared to be some work for the firm. He looked back at me with a smile.

"Hello, Sleepyhead," he said. "How did you sleep?"

"Pretty good," I smiled. I yawned and stretched, thinking of the wonderful way I was put to sleep. "What are you working on?"

"Just helping my dad with some research for a client," he responded. I smiled at him as I breezed by, sliding my fingertips across his broad, bare shoulders before sitting on the steel gray sofa.

"Speaking of work," I smiled. "Dionne and I are going to Open Mic at Exodus Thursday night. Can you come?"

He sighed and dropped his hands to his sides. "I'd love to, Kamila. But I'm swamped with work for the firm."

"I'd really appreciate it if you could be there," I persisted. "This could be really good for Dionne and me. I'd really like to see your handsome face in the audience."

"I'd really like to be there, Babe. I can't."

I released a frustrated sigh as I laid my head back on the couch. "You mean you don't want to."

"Kamila…"

"You don't want to, Jesse," I could feel the frustration burn from my face as I interrupted him. "If Hannah needed a ride to one of her snooty parties, you'd drop everything. You drop everything anytime a Bennett calls but you can never do it for me. Yet you claim you want me to be a Bennett." Jesse paused and spun around in his chair. He rubbed one hand over his perfectly manicured waves and stared at me with a look of exhaustion and defeat.

41

"Kamila, we just had a wonderful evening. This has nothing to do with Hannah. Please don't bring her into this."

"No. This has plenty to do with Hannah. It was her roommate's mouth you used as a dick cozy, correct?"

"Kamila!" His tone shifted from exhaustion to outright annoyance. I knew he didn't like my crude language and I knew that he didn't care for my negative opinions on his pretty-pretty-princess of a sister, Hannah. But I didn't care. As far as I was concerned, a relationship that began between him and me now involved Hannah and her slutty-slut college roommate, Cassandra.

"I'm not going to argue with you about this, Kamila," he continued. "I can't make it to your show. It has nothing to do with Hannah or anyone else in my family. I have to work. I hope that you will come to understand." He closed his laptop and walked back into the bedroom. I could feel the walls shake from the force of the slamming door. I turned the TV on Netflix so I could watch old episodes of *Grey's Anatomy* until I fell asleep on the couch.

The next morning, I was awakened by a soft kiss on my forehead. I opened my eyes to see Jesse standing over me with a Starbucks Iced Latte in his hand. I sat up on the couch and adjusted my nightie.

"Thank you, Babe," I smiled, taking the delicious cup of diabetes from his hand.

"You're welcome. I'm sorry we fought. I don't like us to go to bed angry."

"I don't want to go to bed angry either," I replied, taking a sip of my latte.

"There are some scones on the counter. What do you have planned today?"

"I'll probably do some shopping with Dionne to prep for tomorrow's show. Then we'll just hang out for a while."

"I hate when you go to those south side clubs by yourself," Jesse sighed.

"Jesse, I've lived on the south side for a good chunk of my life. Besides, I won't be alone. Dionne will be there."

"Yes," Jesse laughed. "Dionne's pretty psycho. The two of you should be fine, I suppose." He reached into the back pocket of his gray pleated slacks and pulled out his wallet. Looking inside, he pulled out an American Express card, placing it in my hand.

"Here," he said. "For your show. Treat Dionne and yourself to some cute outfits. On me." I smiled as I took the card from him. This charming, handsome, wealthy man was treating my friend and me to a day of shopping. I was sure he was doing this out of the guilt he probably felt for blowing off my performance, arguing with me, and playing bobbing for apples with Cassie McSlut. At either rate, I was also sure that this gesture would weaken Dionne's desire to cut him for breaking my heart. As for me, the jury was still out.

Chapter Five

The initial plan was to shop near Dionne's apartment on Madison and Pulaski, but once she caught wind of Jesse giving me his American Express card, she insisted we make a day of it and go to Nordstrom on Michigan Avenue. When we were poor little girls from the projects, Big Momma would often bring Dionne and me downtown to window shop on State Street and the Magnificent Mile. She loved taking us to see the window displays at Marshall Field's and Carson's during the holidays and we would go over to the Daley Center to see the huge Christmas tree. Dionne was like the second grandchild Big Momma never had. Almost anything Big Momma did for me, she did for Dionne. We would pretend we could go into any store on Michigan Avenue and buy whatever we wanted. The problem with window shopping came along when we grew to be teenagers. We were no longer

45

seen as cute little brown girls with wonder in our eyes. We were viewed as potential shoplifters from the ghetto. But on this day, in 2018, Dionne and I stood within the stores of Nordstrom with plastic in hand. We could afford not to say, "Just looking."

Dionne immediately became infatuated with a section of scarves in the store. I was sure she likened herself to a distant relative of Erykah Badu the way she could work her way around a scarf. I watched her eyes as they focused on a lavender scarf with little yellow flowers.

"No, Dee," I sighed. "You have a million scarves and I'm sure that 900,000 of them are lavender. I'm not swiping this card on a more expensive version of something you already own."

"Really, Mila?" she replied with a suck of her teeth. "And how many jumpsuits, pantsuits, jean suits, and other uniform outfits do you own?" She pointed out the pale pink jumpsuit I was currently wearing.

"Bitch, I look cute," I laughed, primping my honey blond curls. As we continued teasing each other, a thin, pale woman approached us. Her sandy brown hair was tossed neatly into a bun as she peaked at us over her thick black glasses. Her lips were pursed as she clinched a clipboard close to her chest. She wore a sharply pressed white blouse and navy pants.

"Umm, can I help you?" Dionne placed her hands on her hips as she stared at the woman with narrowed eyes.

"I was simply coming to see if you needed help finding anything," the woman responded with a nervous smile while her eyes appeared to be searching for a silent alarm button. My eyes turned to Dionne, giving her a nod to assure her I had the situation under control. I secretly hoped to myself that Dionne did not pull a razor blade from some secretly hidden crevice and attack this woman who appeared to be in dire need of a veggie burger. I turned my attention to the woman.

"Ma'am," I began. "We're simply looking for an ensemble for a concert we plan on attending with my fiancé, Jesse Bennett, Esquire." I pulled the American Express card from my purse and flashed it at the woman, whose eyes switched from red-alert wide to commission based smizing. For those who are unfamiliar with *America's Next Top Model*, smizing is when one smiles with one's eyes.

"Why of course," the woman exclaimed as tension melted from her face. "What sort of musical event? Is it formal or casual?"

"Oh it's very casual," Dionne mocked in the best haughty-bitch voice she could muster. "I'm looking for a floor-length dress. Something flowy that flatters my curves." She fanned her hands up and down her voluptuous frame while holding her chin in the air. I couldn't help but snicker a bit.

"Indeed," the woman smiled, walking us to the Misses section of the store. Dionne walked up and down the aisles of clothing until her eyes locked with a floor length brown dress with empire sleeves. She smiled as she rushed to the dressing room to try it on.

"What look are you going for?" the woman asked me.

"I'm looking for black palazzo pants and a nice, colorful top," I responded as I searched through the racks of clothing. The woman disappeared and came back with a colorful tunic dress and a pair of strappy black heels.

"I think this would look fabulous on you," she suggested. "I know it's not palazzo pants, but this dress will show off those legs of yours."

"I don't know," I squirmed. "I don't really wear skirts or dresses."

"Why not?" she asked.

"It's a long story." I attempted to feign confidence as I was not about to share my insecurities with a prejudiced stranger.

"EEEEEEK!" The uncomfortable moment with the sales lady was interrupted as Dionne squealed from the dressing room.

"Kamila," she shrieked. "You have to come see!" The woman and I rushed towards the dressing rooms as Dionne emerged. The dress was a perfect fit. The brown hue was a touch darker than Dionne's mocha skin.

"I love it," I exclaimed. "You don't normally wear that color. It looks great on you."

"I take your advice sometimes," she laughed. Her eyes shifted to the tunic dress the saleswoman held in her hands. "Yes, Kamila! Do it, girl!"

I looked back at the dress.

"No, Dionne," I hissed. "You know why."

"Bitch," Dionne snapped. "The only person who notices that is you. You need to let that go. Try on the dress!" Dionne and the saleswoman's eyes widened with affirmation. I shrugged my shoulders in surrender and took the dress from the saleswoman's hands.

Stepping into the dressing room, I stripped my clothes. I cringed as I looked down at my scarred legs from the car accident I was in six years prior. I was struck by a hit and run driver as I sat in a parked car. The accident left me

49

with a broken fibula and pretty nasty gashes that left permanent scars. Since then, the only people who had seen my bare legs were Dionne, Jesse, my mother, and Big Momma.

I studied the top half of my body in the mirror. The fabric clung to me like oil to a canvas. My body tightened with anxiety as my eyes traced the fabric down to my bare legs.

"Open the door, bitch!" Dionne called. She turned her attention to the saleswoman, whispering, "It's okay. We joke this way."

Tension overtook me as I took hesitant steps out of the fitting room. I made a failed attempt at concealing my scars by crossing my right leg over my left.

"Stand up straight and be beautiful, girl!" Dionne commanded. I focused on my breaths, repeating the word, "beautiful" to myself over and over in my mind.

"I think it's gorgeous," the saleswoman gushed. My cheeks became flushed.

"We'll take everything," Dionne commanded, smiling at me. I took in their approving faces and looked down at my legs. I wasn't even sure the saleswoman noticed the scars. *Maybe I was worried about nothing*, I thought to myself.

"Okay, I'll take it," I sighed. I went back to the dressing room and changed back into my clothes.

Dionne and I finalized our purchases and thanked the woman for her assistance. We took the blue line back to her house where my car was parked because I refused to drive in downtown Chicago traffic. I was proud of Dionne and myself for stepping outside the box and trying something different. I purchased an above knee dress for the night's performance but Jesse wouldn't even be there to see it. I felt triumphant and disappointed at the same time.

***

The next night, Dionne and I arrived at Exodus nightclub for open mic. The warm night sky was illuminated by the street lights and neon signs of nearby bars and shops. Eclectic artists and people seeking a good time filed the streets, walking in and out of the club. We entered the room which was packed with poets, singers, and musicians. Case's *Touch Me, Tease Me* blared on the speakers as acts lined up in front of the sign-in sheet. Dionne and I jumped in line to sign up. That's when I heard it.

"My, my, my. If it ain't my Mila," a familiar voice sang behind me. The hairs on my arm stood in formation as I recognized the voice.

Demarcus.

Chapter Six

Demarcus stood behind me looking sexier than I last remembered. He stood with confidence, wearing a white, tight-fitted V-neck T-shirt that hugged his perfect, chiseled chest. He wore a black vest and black pants that hung loosely over his Timberland boots. His deep brown eyes dazzled and sparkled as the club lights danced atop his curly black hair. The last time I saw that man, I hated the ground he walked on. But tonight, for some unknown reason, I found myself staring at my high school crush like he was a caramel buffet that was made just for me.

I stood with my lips parted, trying to think of a word to say.

"Cruz!" Dionne exclaimed, pushing past me and gripping him in a tight hug. "Last time I saw you, you were running from the cops! Where have you been?"

"Moms sent me to live with my pops' family in Florida during my senior year," he responded. "I've been living down in St. Petersburg but Moms wasn't feeling too good so I came back home to check on things." He moved his focus from Dionne to me, licking his lips as he looked me up and down like a dog longing for a bone.

"But, what's good with you, Mila?" he asked.

"Just living life," I responded, smiling so hard that my cheeks wanted to run from my face. *Why was I smiling?*

"I feel you, Ma," he replied. "So you here to watch the talent?"

"We *are* the talent," Dionne exclaimed as she wrapped her arm around me.

"Oh yeah?" he asked.

"You sound surprised," I responded. "I was writing songs back when we were together."

"I don't remember that," Demarcus said, rubbing his hand over his curls.

"I do," I replied. "Maybe you're just getting old." I spun on my heels to walk away, quickly remembering the boy who broke my heart. He reached out to grab my arm with the "whose pussy is this" sort of force that used to make me melt back when he almost took my virginity.

"Hold on, baby girl," he smiled and I turned to look at him. I shuddered as I looked down at his grip on my wrist.

"Um, Demarcus?" I uttered.

"Yeah, baby?"

"I got a man," I said, quickly regaining my composure. I pulled my arm from his grip and walked across the room. Dionne quickly ran behind me.

"What was that?" she asked.

"What?"

"You know what," she smiled. "That exchange with Cruz."

"I don't know what you're talking about," I gave a dismissive shrug.

"Lies! You spent years fussing over that man and you've spent days fussing over Jesse and the baby drinker and now you're over here drooling over Cruz."

"I know," I admitted. "I don't know what happened. I don't want Demarcus."

"You sure about that?" Dionne asked, pursing her lips.

54

"I'm sure," I replied. I wasn't sure if either of us believed my words.

Over the loudspeakers, we could hear the host's voice. "Up next to the stage; Karma!" Applause rang throughout the room while Dionne and I regained our focus and rushed to the stage. The bass from Dionne's instrumental vibrated the wooden stage as the two of us stepped up to the microphone. I stared at the pale orange wall at the back of the room as I lost myself in the music.

I can't believe it/ My heart lays in tiny pieces

I normally don't show weakness/ But here I sit defeated

How could you do this? / Why didn't you choose us?

Now I'm all confused/ But yet I still love you

Sweeping pieces of my heart from the floor

I gave you all I could but you still wanted more

In a tug of war between wanting and rage

I thought that I'd be in your arms for all my days

How could you push away my love?

How could you push away my love?

Dionne gripped the microphone for her verse.

Flames of rage in me, burning red and orange

Heat takes over me, is this what you want?

I would have given you all but this is what you do

It's gonna take armed guards to keep me off of you

I've left my flowers on the grave that is our love

The grieving time has passed, so no I won't be thinking of you

You got me all the way messed up

In a tug of war between wanting and rage

I thought that I'd be in your arms for all my days

How could you push away my love?

How could you push away my love?

The audience applauded as the song approached its end. I returned from the outer body experience I went into while performing and looked over to Dionne, who was beaming with excitement. The song appeared to be a success despite the craziness I had been going through with Jesse.

"Girl!" Dionne exclaimed as we left the stage. "You're like Mary J Blige with that heartbreak shit! I told you to use that pain!" I rubbed my hands through my curls as I let out a nervous laugh. As we continued gushing over the performance, I felt a presence standing behind me.

"If I didn't know any better, I'd think you were talking about me, Mila." Demarcus. As I turned to face him, he smiled at me while biting his bottom lip with a quiet cockiness.

"Well I wasn't," I replied, struggling as hard as I could to appear unbothered. *What was I doing?* "That was so long ago."

"Well if you weren't talking about me, then who?"

"Demarcus, I haven't talked to you in years. Plus you're my ex. Do you really think that I'm going to start pouring my heart out to you?"

"You used to," he said, lowering his eyes. I could see sadness peeking through his usual bravado.

"Yes, used to. Before you started pouring your dick into Janette."

"By the way," Dionne chimed in. "Did you ever get tested after that? I mean I love you, Cruz, but her coochie hair got bed bugs. I don't know what you were thinking about."

Dionne and I snickered as Demarcus attempted to hide the hurt I could clearly see on his face. Although I hadn't seen or spoken to him in years, I knew him. I knew him well enough to know that his eyes were saying what his lips wouldn't.

I pulled Dionne to the side. "Let me talk to him," I whispered.

"About what?" Dionne exclaimed loud enough to be heard across the Illinois/Indiana state line.

"Just let me talk to him," I insisted. She gave me a hesitant, annoyed glare before walking away.

"What's going on, Demarcus?" I asked. He glanced at me for a moment before attempting to regain his usual shell of fake confidence.

"I don't know what you're talking about," he shrugged.

"Save it for someone who doesn't know you," I fussed.

He paced over to the steps that led to the stage. The last act was done and Faith Evans' *Love like This* boomed across the room. People stood from their seats and clamored to the middle of the dance floor while my eyes focused on the man who was once the air I breathed. Ten years had passed since we were an item, and I had been with Jesse for three, but I was still familiar with this man as if we hadn't missed a day.

"Now what's going on?" I sighed, attempting to carry my voice over the music.

"What's not going on?" he responded. "Moms is sick, I blew it with you…"

"Demarcus, that was so long ago," I replied. In my mind, I knew he'd want to talk about us. A part of me longed to hear him out. But our time had passed. I belonged to Jesse.

"I know, I know," he said. "I'm not trying to step on your toes, Mila. I know you're occupied at the moment. It's just…"

"Just?"

"Kamila, I miss you. I mean we were all friends. You, Dionne, me, Janette, Lorenzo… I understand that I messed up but it seems like I lost all of y'all because of it."

I sighed. As much as I wanted to be difficult about it, he was right. Demarcus and I had been friends since he moved on our block when I was eleven. When I was about fifteen, we decided to start dating. We knew we had feelings for each other but I was hesitant to start a relationship with a friend. We promised each other if anything were to go wrong, we would work to maintain our friendship.

Two years into the relationship, Demarcus was being the typical teenage boy. His hormones were setting off fire alarms but I wouldn't go further than letting him finger me when no one else was looking. Of course, I wanted Demarcus to be my first. But I refused to repeat my mother's mistakes. On the other hand, Janette had been sexually active since the eighth grade and her specialty was other girls' boyfriends. She took pictures of Demarcus sleeping in her bed and sent them to my phone. It broke my heart. Dionne was my best friend, so she sided with me. Janette was a hoe who wanted to be turned into a housewife so her relationship with Demarcus died before it began. Demarcus's older brother Lorenzo was serving time in Dixon for riding in a car with some boys who killed somebody. As angry as I had been with him, it was then I realized Demarcus had lost all of his friends over a mistake he made when he was seventeen. I was still living with Jesse after his indiscretion and he was a grown ass man.

I sighed as I plopped down on the steps next to him. "I guess I did promise," I said.

"We promised," he smiled. "And I fucked up."

"You did."

"I know. And I want to make it right. No disrespect to dude, but y'all were my friends. Moms not doing too well, Lorenzo's not here. I need y'all."

I let his words linger in my mind. I was doubtful that Jesse would be okay with me being friends with my ex-boyfriend, but Demarcus was right. We were all friends and he really didn't have anyone left.

"The bar's about to close," Dionne said, interrupting my train of thought. "I'm ready to go."

"Hold on," I replied.

"I gotta work in the morning," she insisted. "Later Cruz!" She smiled at Demarcus before grabbing my arm and pulling me towards the door.

"What is wrong with you?" I snapped.

"Nothing," she responded. "I'm helping you."

We walked out into the parking lot to my car and hopped inside. Erykah Badu's *Other Side of the Game* played through the car speakers. Dionne put on her seatbelt and glared at me, crossing her arms.

"What?" I asked.

"What, yourself?" she responded. "What were you doing with Cruz?"

"I was talking to him. We were all friends at some point, Dee. He misses us."

"Misses us? Or misses you?"

"Us! He knows I got a man."

"Girl, you stupid as hell. When has that ever stopped a man from wanting to get what he felt was his?"

"What he felt was his?" I laughed. "I'm not a basketball, Dee."

"Maybe not, Mi," Dionne responded. "But he's sure trying to slam dunk into that ass."

***

I took Dionne home and headed to my apartment. My mind flooded with thoughts and emotions. The performance. The dress. My scars. Jesse. He missed everything. I wanted to share this with him. And Demarcus. He was still fine and truthfully, I hoped that Dionne was right. I wanted him to miss me because I missed him. But why did I miss him? I shouldn't have been missing him. I was with Jesse. Jesse.

As I parked the car, I decided to center my thoughts on Jesse. He hadn't seen me in a dress in years and I wanted to tell him about my performance. I shook away all thoughts of Demarcus as I walked up the steps to the apartment. I wanted to be excited. I needed to feel excited. But as I stepped closer to the front door, memories flashed in my mind. The back of Jesse's head. The weave between his legs. Me, wielding a baseball bat. Looking out into the crowd and not seeing Jesse's face. I wanted to feel excited but my body flooded with depression, anger, and sadness. As I put my key in the door, I prayed silently that Jesse would be asleep.

He wasn't.

He sat at the island bar, smiling at me as I walked through the door. He took a sip of brandy and put it down.

"How was the show?" he asked.

"It was fine," I shrugged.

"Just fine?"

"Yes. Just fine. I'm going to bed."

Chapter Seven - Demarcus

Demarcus beamed as he walked through the automatic doors to the Glynn Lakes Assisted Living Home. He walked through the lobby to the front desk, where a short chubby woman who appeared to be in her fifties peered over her glasses while reading an issue of *Redbook*. Demarcus leaned his elbow on top of the desk.

"How you doing, Mrs. Willis?" he asked.

"Oh, I'm doing just fine, baby," she smiled through the creases on her sienna-colored face. "You seem to be in good spirits today."

"I'm on top of the world. How's my girl doing today?"

"She's been okay. She's been sleeping a lot since her last treatment but so far so good. You know, we gotta be on point with Ms. Jones because we know you're going to make sure she's okay. I sure do admire how you take such good care of your momma."

"I'm just repaying the favor," Demarcus responded. "I owe her this." He signed in on the visitor's list and walked down the long corridor to the end of the hall, where his mother's room was located. Denise laid with her bed elevated, watching an old episode of *Walker, Texas Ranger*. Her thin gray hair was hidden underneath a black and white scarf as she clutched the hospital remote in her frail hands. She turned towards her youngest boy and flashed him a weak smile.

"It's good to see your face," she said.

"It's always good to see yours," he responded, taking a seat in the green chair beside her bed. "How are you feeling?"

"Great now that you're here. How's my boy?"

"I'm great now that I can see that smile. I found her, Momma."

"Oh that's so great, baby," Denise said, sitting up in bed. "I know that's been on your mind for quite some time."

"I just hate that I messed up with her," he responded. "Now she's with somebody else." Demarcus looked down at his lap. His smile began to fade a bit at the thought of Kamila being in the arms of another man. She was his first love. She was his only love and he never recovered from breaking her heart by sleeping with Janette. He knew Kamila didn't trust Janette, but Janette was a quick fix to a temporary problem. At the time, he felt that he was just being a man.

"Well is she married to the man?" Denise asked.

"No, but it's pretty serious," he responded.

"Well, who knows? Don't count yourself out just yet. And if nothing else, you can at least talk to her and make peace with that situation."

"You're right," he nodded.

"You know, I may not have much time left," Denise continued. "I don't want you to be alone when I go." Tears began to form in Demarcus's eyes as Denise reached out to rub his face with her delicate hands.

"I don't want to think about you leaving me," he whimpered.

"We've talked about this, son," she responded. "I don't have much time. I'm just glad you're here to spend this time with me now. We've lost so much already."

"I know. Much of that is my fault."

"You hush that," Denise said. "You were a little boy. You gotta forgive yourself." Demarcus sat back in the chair as tears began to stream down his face.

"You know, when I was back in Florida and I got that phone call, I blamed myself."

"Blamed yourself for what?" Denise snapped.

"You know, Momma."

"For me getting cancer? Boy, stop that."

"Momma, we lived a rough life and I was a nightmare. Me and Zo both."

Demarcus thought back to his troubled life with his family. He was born in St. Petersburg, Florida to an African-American mother and a Dominican father. His father, Alfonso was abusive to him, his older brother, Lorenzo, and his mother until he was five years old. Becoming tired of the abuse, Denise took her children and fled to her hometown of Chicago, moving in with her older sister until she got on her feet. Witnessing the violence between his parents and being uprooted from his childhood home had a negative effect on both boys, causing them to act out. They would get suspended often for fighting and disrespecting teachers and would often lash out at their mother when she would try to intervene. As they got older, they started ditching class to hang out with the GDs around the neighborhood. When Demarcus was a freshman in high school, Lorenzo was sentenced to 25 years in prison for being in a car during a drive-by shooting. During his junior year, Demarcus was nearly sent to jail himself after being caught joyriding in a stolen vehicle. Having had enough, Denise made the tough decision of sending Demarcus back to Florida, feeling that she didn't want to lose another son to prison, and hoping that having a male influence in Demarcus' life could get him back on track.

While living with his father, Demarcus began to understand the hardships his mother went through when he was younger. He remembered the beatings his father would give the family. During his last days of high school, his father came home drunk from the bar he would often frequent and started a fight with Demarcus, forcing Demarcus to knock him out cold.

Ashamed to return to Chicago with his mother and refusing to live with his father, Demarcus alternated his time between living in homeless shelters, with high school friends, and with temporary girlfriends. He was eventually able to go to trade school and learned to operate a forklift, which helped him get on his feet and establish himself. He was able to get his own apartment and a car.

One day, when coming home from work, Demarcus got a call from his aunt, Celia that shook him to his core.

"Demarcus," she cried.

"What's going on, Auntie?"

"It's Denise. She collapsed in church the other day and we took her to the hospital. The doctor says its stage 4 bone cancer. It's spread to her heart and lungs."

Demarcus dropped the phone and fell to the floor in tears. His one and only mother was now staring in the face of a deadly disease and it was not looking good. He had spent years resenting her and more years hiding and feeling ashamed for how he treated her but at that moment, all he wanted to do was be with his mom and take care of her the way she tried to take care of him. He knew that excessive stress could lead to cancer. He wondered if his father contributed to her condition. He wondered if he or Lorenzo caused the illness. He couldn't be sure, but he was sure he wanted to be there to help.

The next day, Demarcus turned in his resignation at work and drove 23 hours from St. Petersburg to Chicago. Together with his aunt, Celia, they decided to put Denise into an assisted living facility so she could receive around-the-clock care. He moved back to his childhood home where he lived with his mom before moving to Florida.

"Why didn't you tell me sooner?" he asked Denise.

"I didn't want you to worry," she responded. "I didn't want any of you to worry. I thought I would have this thing beat before I'd ever had to say a word."

"But I could have come here sooner," he groaned. Denise reached toward him, wiping a tear from his cheek.

"What could you have done, Demarcus?" she asked. "You'd just sit around and watch me get sick."

"But I would have been here." His chest grew heavy with grief as he thought over all the time he missed with his mother.

"You're here now," she said. "We can't do nothing about what we think we should have done in the past. All we have is today." He gently grabbed her hand from his face and held it.

"I love you, lady," he whispered.

"I love you too," Denise responded. "And I want you to get out here and live your life. If you want to work things out with Kamila, you do that. If not, I want you to get out there and meet you somebody so you won't have to be alone crying over me. I want you to have me some grandbabies. And if you have a girl, you can give her my name as a middle name. Don't make her first name Denise. People don't name their children that anymore and I don't want my grandbaby growing up with an old lady name."

"You're not old," he smiled.

"The hell you lie," she laughed. "But it's nothing wrong with getting older. I lived a full life. I know you see the bad things, but I see the blessings that have come out of those bad things. Had I never met your father, I wouldn't have this beautiful boy sitting in front of me. You have been wonderful since you've been back in town. You've grown into a fine young man. I'm proud to be able to call you my son."

Demarcus smiled at his mother's words. He had thought many things of himself throughout the years, but he never thought of himself with pride. He lashed out at his mother and hurt Kamila partially because deep within himself, he felt unworthy of love. When his father would beat him during his drunken fits of rage, he would wonder what horrible things he had done to deserve what he was receiving. He thought that he and his mother both had to be horrible people to deserve the punishments his father would dish out. He thought his father would know horrible when he recognized it because he was horrible himself.

Demarcus sat back and watched TV with his mother until she drifted off to sleep. He stood from his chair and leaned over her, kissing her on her forehead as he lowered her bed back to lying position. He covered her with blankets and took the remote from her hand, turning the television off and placing the remote back beside her. He walked back down the corridor to the desk where Mrs. Willis sat, working on a crossroad puzzle.

"Don't work too hard now," he smiled as he passed her by.

"Child, I'm gonna do my best," she responded.

As Demarcus walked through the automatic doors and to his car, his heart flooded with warm feelings as his mother's words ran through his mind. He was happy that if nothing else, he was able to return home and do some good in her life while she was still alive to see it. Deep down, he hoped he'd be able to walk back into her room hand-in-hand with the love of his life. He wanted her to see him in love and happy so she wouldn't need to worry about him in the afterlife. He wanted her to see him in love and happy with Kamila because that was all he ever wanted since he was a child.

As he sat in his car, his mind wandered back to the night before at the club. Seeing Kamila stirred up all the love he carried for her since he was 14 years old. She still looked just as beautiful as he remembered, except her relaxed, shoulder-length, dark hair was now natural and blond. He thought of her smile – the smile he took away from her when she saw the pictures of him with Janette. His stomach turned as he imagined some mystery man hugging and kissing the woman he loved. He thought to himself that as long as she was happy, he would try to make peace with the fact of her no longer being with him. He didn't want to accept it, but he would have rather had her as a friend than not have her in his life at all.

Chapter Eight

It was Friday night and the Bulls were playing against the Spurs. I rushed up the stairs to the third floor, fully aware that Silas would have had my head if I missed watching the game with him. Thankfully I only missed five minutes after tip-off when I arrived. I gagged for a moment at the strong scent of Silas's cigarettes as I entered the room.

"You late, Baby Girl!" he teased.

"Any time I arrive is on time, Old Man," I replied. I moved with brisk steps into the living room, taking a seat on the burgundy recliner across from my uncle. The Bulls were off to a great start, whooping the Spurs 4-0. Silas had ordered my favorite pizza from Giordano's – deep dish sausage and spinach, with a two-liter Coke. Next to his feet sat four out of a six-pack of Miller Genuine Draft, Silas' favorite beer since back when he would steal from Big Momma's stash as a teen. One can lay crumpled next to the other cans while he held the last one in his hand.

"We off to a good start," Silas proclaimed.

"I see," I replied. I didn't really care about sports but it was the way I bonded with Silas. Once he was over the initial shock of Momma's pregnancy, he hoped she would have a boy to balance out the estrogen-filled family. Much of my baby gear was Bears, Bulls, and White Sox gear. Once the Blackhawks started winning, we began to take a fair-weather interest in hockey. The games would bore me, but I got to spend time with Silas and talk to him about what would be going on in my life. He always gave the best advice, and at that moment, I needed the natural calm that was Silas. Jesse and I were barely speaking and I found myself thinking more and more about Demarcus. I couldn't admit it to Silas, though. He always said he was never wrong and I was not trying to confirm that.

"I thought I saw your car out front," Momma said, flinging the door open to Silas' apartment. "You could have told me you were here."

"Hi Momma," I said. My momma and I were like oil and water and truthfully, I knew she was home. I had hoped she was asleep or on her way out so I wouldn't have had to cross her path. But there she was, crossing mine.

"Hi Momma," she mocked. "You act like you can't speak to your own momma. What y'all doing?"

"Watching the game," Silas interjected. "So either come on over and sit down and shut up or go back downstairs." He winked at me. I smiled.

"You ain't gotta be so rude about it," Momma responded, shifting her burgundy wig. "I'm about to head out anyway. I just came up to say hi. What you got going on tomorrow night?"

"Nunya," Silas teased. "Why?"

"You ain't got nothing planned you old fool," Momma teased. "What about you, Mila?"

"I'm going out of town tomorrow," I responded.

"Aw, you and Jesse going out?" she asked, taking a seat next to Silas.

"No, me and Dionne."

"Well, where y'all going? Maybe you'll get back in time. I want you to meet somebody." *Probably a new boyfriend*, I thought to myself. Suddenly I was happy to be driving Dionne to a maximum security prison.

"I may stay over in a hotel, depending on what time we're done. I'm driving Dionne downstate." Momma paused as her expression shifted from playful probing to slight dread.

"Downstate where?"

"Does it matter? Why are you pushing this so hard, Momma? I'm almost thirty."

Momma stood up from the couch and began pacing back and forth in front of Silas while twisting her hair around her fingers.

"What if something happens to you, Kamila? I think your family should know where you're going."

"I'm taking Dionne to visit her dad since it's so important for you to know."

"Why do you need to do that?" she asked, her voice rising an octave as the color began to fade from her face.

"Because she asked me, and because I'm free," I responded, standing to my feet. I felt a sudden overwhelm at the tension that was forming in the room.

"I really want you to come to dinner tomorrow and bring Jesse," she persisted. "Come on, Kamila. I don't ask you for much. Dionne's a grown ass woman. Why do you have to take her?"

"I'm not coming and I'm certainly not bringing Jesse. Let it go, Momma."

"Kamila…"

"Let… it… go."

I grabbed my purse, stomping down the stairs and out of the building. As I walked towards my car, I saw a familiar face approaching me.

"My, my, my, if it ain't my Mila." Demarcus.

"What are you doing over here?" I asked. It wasn't the right time to run into Demarcus. I was white hot with anger from my mom and ice cold with indifference towards Jesse. With the way I was feeling, I could have collapsed into Demarcus's broad chest like I used to do when we were together.

"I was in the area," he responded. "What about you?"

"Same, but I'm leaving now."

"Why so soon?"

"I gotta get home to Jesse," I said, avoiding eye contact.

"Come on and hang out with me for a little bit," he said, twirling his fingers around mine. I could feel the glisten between my legs. *What was I doing?* I pulled my hand away from his.

"What are you doing?" I said with a nervous laugh. "You know I have a man!"

He nodded and placed his hands at his sides. "You're right, Ma. No disrespect. Let's just get some dinner."

"I just ate."

"Well, you can watch me eat while we catch up," he laughed. "We're friends, remember?"

"We're friends."

We decided to walk to De 'Arco's on 63rd Street so he could get the big ass pizza puff that he'd been ordering since high school. As we walked through the night wind, we engaged in a bit of conversation.

"So how are things with old dude?" he asked.

"Jesse and I are fine."

"Sure you are," he laughed. "If that song wasn't about me, it was about somebody." I blushed. As well as I felt I still knew him, he surely still knew me.

"Even if we weren't," I responded, trying to regain my composure. "What makes you think I would tell you?"

"You don't have to," he smiled. As we continued walking, we crossed paths with a man who looked as if he hadn't had a bath or a nonalcoholic drink in quite some time. I met eyes with him before looking away, silently thanking God that I wasn't walking around alone. The man stopped in front of Demarcus and me and flashed a smile. The teeth that remained in his mouth were coated with thick rings of black that faded into a dark yellowish color.

"Wassup, shawty," the man smiled. There it was. The street harassment I loved oh so much. I became increasingly relieved that Demarcus was there with me, although this guy didn't seem like very much of a threat. He actually looked pretty harmless, sort of like a hood jester, but even hood jesters could be dangerous and I was not willing to take that chance.

"You looking good, Shawty!" he grumbled, looking me up and down.

"Umm… thank you?" I responded. Demarcus wrapped his arm around my waist and pulled me closer.

"Thank you," Demarcus chimed in, passing me a reassuring look. I exhaled with relief.

"Y'all not together," the man laughed.

"We are," I smiled. *Why was I lying? Why did I like his touch around my waist?*

"Prove it," the man said. *What was this dude, some type of freak?* I thought to myself. I stood in place with my lips slightly parted, amazed at the audacity of this strange man. As my mind flooded with thoughts, trying to understand what was happening, Demarcus leaned over to me, pressing his lips against mine. *Wait!* He held his position, pulling me closer with his hand against the small of my back. My mind screamed for me to resist but my lips had a mind of their own. They parted, welcoming his tongue. *I should be stopping this. But I want it.* I wrapped my arms around him and lost myself in his kiss. A few moments passed and I opened my eyes to see if the man bought our rouse as much as I seemed to be buying it. He was gone.

I pushed away from Demarcus and stared at him as nervousness flooded my being.

"What are we doing?" I asked.

"I don't know," he breathed. We stood on the sidewalk, staring into each other's eyes. His breath was heavy. My breath was heavy. My mind screamed for me to turn and run back to my car. My mind wanted me to go home to Jesse. *I am not this girl.*

"You wanna go somewhere so we can talk alone?" he asked.

Say no! Say no! "Yes."

***

Denise's house looked just how I remembered it. Pink carpet with a white sofa set that was covered with pink roses. The couches were wrapped in plastic. A clear glass bowl of peppermint candy sat on top of a white coffee table. Although Demarcus's mother had been in the hospital for quite some time, the air still smelled of her Little Red Dress perfume.

I stepped inside ahead of Demarcus as he took the key out of the door. I felt his touch on my back as I looked around the room. I slowly turned to him and we immediately picked up where we started on the street. We traded fervent kisses as he guided me through the living room to his old bedroom. I sat on the bed and stared at him with wanting as he stripped from his clothes. There I sat in the very same room where we used to have our make-out sessions. Any hint of my inner voice of reason seemed to have packed up and left for vacation because all I could think about was mounting that man.

I stood up and slid out of my sneakers and blue jeans. I walked around him and shoved him onto the bed. I mounted him and guided his shaft into me. My body burned with passion as I rocked my hips and bounced on him. I knew I shouldn't have been there. I knew I shouldn't have been doing what I was doing but I was there. I was doing it. Doing him. I only wanted to feel passion. I didn't want to think of Jesse or Momma. I didn't even want to think about Demarcus, but… Ooooh, Demarcus!

He picked me up and flipped me onto my back. He pushed my legs over my head and thrust every single bit of himself into me. Every move he made gave me a delicious amount of hurt. He moaned in my ear and whispered my name.

"Kamila..."

I couldn't say it. Although I was in his bed, although I had already crossed that line and was already on the same level as Demarcus and Jesse, I couldn't say his name. For some reason, that was the deal breaker. I had another man inside of me but saying that man's name was the deal breaker.

Jesse.

Suddenly, the heat simmered. Demarcus continued his motion, but all I could think about was Jesse. I was being a complete bitch to him over getting head and now, I was in another man's bed with my legs over my head.

"Stop," I said.

"Why?" Demarcus asked as he slowed without completely stopping.

"This isn't right... Jesse..."

"Its fine, Mila," he panted. "He did the same thing to you. Hell, you forgave him and stayed with him. You didn't give me that chance."

"I was a kid, Demarcus," I sighed as I sat up and pushed him off of me.

83

"So was I."

"That was the past."

"But here you are." He was right. I was in his bed half naked. My mind told me after the first kiss to leave but nooooo. I had to listen to my pussy instead.

"Yeah, but I shouldn't be." I got up to get dressed.

"Come on, Kamila," Demarcus insisted. "Can we talk about it?"

"We've talked enough."

Chapter Nine

What just happened? What did I do? How could I? My mind raced with thoughts as I drove down the Dan Ryan expressway through the late night traffic. I spent years hating Demarcus for messing around with Janette and although I decided to stay with Jesse, I had emotionally cut myself off from him at this point. All the tears I cried and the many times I said I would never do to anyone what they had done to me and there I was. I did the same thing to Jesse. At that point, I no longer had the right to be angry or self-righteous. *Maybe if I came clean with him, we could call it even and he'd forgive me. Maybe he would hate me.* Many scenarios played through my mind, but I didn't know for sure what would happen.

On the other hand, as guilty as I felt about it, being with Demarcus felt good. It felt familiar and comfortable. We hadn't missed a beat with each other. He knew my heartbeat.

He knew my body. He knew me. But I was in a committed relationship with Jesse and I felt the need to honor that, although I hadn't. But neither did Jesse.

I arrived home to my Lincoln Park apartment. Jesse was home. I had hoped to get lucky that he'd already been asleep. I walked up the stairs with a trepidation I hadn't felt since I was a kid on the way home to one of Big Momma's ass whoopings. I opened the door to the apartment and looked around. The kitchen and living room were covered with lit candles while K-Ci and Jojo's *All My Life* played on the stereo. On the island bar sat two plates of food joined by one wine glass. Jesse stood in front of the bar, holding out the second glass of wine for me.

"Welcome home," he smiled. "I thought you would never make it."

"I did," I responded with a nervous smile. *All this time, I've begged him to try and he wanted to do this now?*

"I made dinner. Salmon, wild rice, and cauliflower." *Not only did he try, he made my favorite. Damn him!*

I took a seat at the bar and joined him for dinner. Jesse was an amazing cook. He learned from his aunt who owned a soul food restaurant. I melted as I took eager bites of pure deliciousness.

"Thank you for dinner," I said.

"It's the least I could do," he responded. "I hate how things have been with us lately. I want us back. Jesse and Kamila."

"I want us back too," I replied. *But did I really?* "I don't wanna fight anymore, Jesse." I took another bite of salmon as he put his fork on his plate. He studied my face for a moment.

"What's on your…" Before I could finish my sentence, he leaped from his seat, pressing his lips to mine. I could feel burning heat from his kisses as he moaned heavily. He wanted me. He did all of this for me but I couldn't. Not now. Not after… Demarcus.

"Hold on, Babe," I said, trying to pull from his embrace. "Let me grab a shower or something."

"No," he commanded. "I need you now." He kissed me again, standing me from the stool and unbuttoning my pants. *Oh no…* He dropped my pants to the floor. Then my panties. Then his pants. He picked me up and placed me back on the stool. He spread my legs and… There it was. Deep passionate strokes as he kissed me all over. The deepness of his voice caused an enticing vibration as he moaned in my ear. I tried to enjoy the love that was being made. My body heaved and tingled from the delicious sting but all I could think about was just two hours prior, it was Demarcus who was making me sweat and moan. I was a total hypocrite but I couldn't tell Jesse. Not now.

"What's wrong?" he asked as he slowed his motion, looking into my eyes.

"Nothing," I lied, blinking the tears from my eyes. "I just love you."

"I love you too," he smiled as he continued his motion. "We... will... get... through... this..."

I moaned. I cried. I wanted to enjoy him. I also wanted to stop and tell him the truth, but all I did was cry. I cried as I accepted the love I wasn't sure I wanted to make. But I was his.

When we were done, I walked into the bathroom and stared at my reflection in the mirror. I ran the shower as I slipped out of the rest of my clothes. I stepped into the tub and curled into a ball, mixing my tears with the water. I was always a person who tried to do the right thing and there I was, having slept with two men in the same night. In many ways, this was worse than anything Demarcus or Jesse had ever done to me and to make matters worse, I let Jesse sleep with me without telling him that I slept with Demarcus. I felt horrible.

"Babe?" Jesse called, minutes later as he entered the bathroom. "You okay? You've been in here for a while." I couldn't bring myself to say words.

Jesse walked into the bathroom and pulled back the shower curtain. I sat at the edge of the tub, shivering with my arms wrapped around my knees as the water had turned cold. He turned off the water and wrapped me in a towel.

"We will be okay," he whispered, kissing my forehead. He had no idea just how far from okay we were.

***

The sun greeted my sleepless eyes as I laid restless in bed. I got up and dressed in jeans and a white tee, covering that with the oversized Bulls sweatshirt I borrowed from Silas. I left Jesse in his slumber as I left the apartment, hopped in the car and put on Jay-Z's *444* album. I took Lake Shore Drive to the 290, heading to Dionne's apartment. When I arrived, Dionne sat on the front steps, dressed in gray sweatpants and a black t-shirt. Her curls peeked out from an ebony head wrap.

"Girl, you look like you didn't sleep at all," she said as she got in the car. "Late night with Jesse?"

"Something like that," I mumbled. I got back on the 290 headed east to the Dan Ryan as *Kill Jay Z* blared over the speakers. Dionne stared at me with intense curiosity as Google Maps interrupted the music, directing the way to our destination.

"Something ain't right," Dionne snapped, adjusting the volume on the car stereo. "What's wrong with you?"

"I don't know what you mean," I lied.

"Girl, give that foolishness to someone who doesn't know you." She laughed. She was right. She knew me better than almost anybody. There was no way I could get away with lying to her and I needed to tell someone.

I gazed down the road, watching as the high rises and shopping centers quickly gave way to cows and cornfields. I felt tears in the lining of my stomach as the truth ate me alive.

I took a deep, hesitant breath. "I did something last night."

"What?" she asked, turning towards me. The words struggled in my throat.

"I slept with Demarcus." I took a quick glance at her to gauge her reaction. She looked at me with a combination of shock and amusement.

"Say something," I said.

"I kind of knew something like this would happen," she responded.

"How?" I asked. "I didn't even know."

"Girl, come on! The way you looked at him when we were at Exodus? How you wanted me to leave you two alone so you could talk? You spent years telling me you had nothing to say to that man but the second you got in front of him, your panties got all wet." I blushed a bit. I didn't want to admit it, but she was right.

"It gets worse," I sighed.

"How?"

"I slept with Jesse right after." I cringed.

"Girl..." she gasped. "What are you doing, taking classes from Janette?"

"I know, I know!" I whined. "I feel so terrible. I tried to tell Jesse no but he wasn't hearing it."

"Of course he wasn't hearing it," she responded. "Those are his goods. No wonder you got that look on your face like you just took a walk of shame."

"You're not helping, Dionne."

"It's not much I can do to help, hoe." She laughed and poked at me so I couldn't help but laugh as well.

"Seriously," Dionne continued. "You need to figure out what's going on between you and Cruz. If I can see there's something still there, I know he can. And if something is still there, you're gonna need to figure out what you're gonna do about your relationship with Jesse."

"I know," I muttered. Before running into Demarcus that night at Exodus, I was sure I was over him. Before that night, I was sure I was ready to work things out with Jesse and even become Mrs. Jesse Bennett but right then, I worried that Jesse and I would never be the same again. And I worried that I was to blame.

"Put it this way," Dionne laughed. "Now all three of you are dirty stinking cheaters. You're even." She was right. No more moral superiority from me.

***

Hours passed before we arrived at the prison. There were walls and barbed wires all over the place with guards everywhere. I was shocked that Dionne asked me to take her to see her dad in the first place as she knew I had a crippling phobia of prisons. Perhaps it was because of the countless hours of *Unsolved Mysteries* and *America's Most Wanted* that Big Momma had me watching as a kid or the *Lockup* marathons I'd watch as an adult, but I had a recurring fear of being stabbed to death in prison. Although I agreed to drive Dionne to see her dad since her license was revoked, I had no intention whatsoever of going inside, which was why I made sure to bring along a few books so I could wait in the car.

"Have a good visit with your dad," I smiled as I parked the car.

"You're not going to sit in this car the whole time," she said. "You can come in with me."

"I don't need to do that. Visit with your dad."

"Kamila, no. You drove all the way down here. I'm not going to leave you sitting in this car. You've never actually met my dad. You can at least come in and say hello."

I gave her a look of annoyance as I got out of the car. We walked together to the front gate as I attempted to come up with some reason why I couldn't go inside with her.

"Don't they have visitor's lists or something?" I asked.

"I already had you put on the list," she replied. The heffa had this planned out all along. I was stuck.

We showed our IDs to the guard at the front gate and emptied our pockets for security check. The inside of the prison didn't have any windows, traces of sunlight or any sign of outside life. We were led into a room filled with visitors. Siblings, cousins, friends, parents, and mothers with screaming babies sat in chairs in front of thick windows, waiting for their incarcerated loved ones to appear on the other side. Dionne's dad was in maximum security prison and wasn't allowed physical contact with visitors. By this time, I knew he had killed someone but I didn't ask for many details and Dionne didn't talk about it much.

As we sat in the chairs, Dionne's dad was led into the visiting area by one guard as another stood at the door. He wore a yellow jumpsuit as the accompanying guard removed his handcuffs. His head was shaved and he wore a salt and pepper mustache and beard. Dionne smiled like a kid on Christmas as she picked up the telephone to talk to her father.

"Hey, Daddy!" she smiled. "How are they treating you in here?"

"Not bad," he said. "Sometimes they forget to leave the mint on my pillow but it's not a big deal." They shared a laugh.

"I'm glad you still keep your sense of humor," Dionne replied with a hint of sadness painting her voice.

"Aww, Peaches. It's largely because of you. Your visits and your letters keep my spirits up in here. How's your momma?"

"She's doing okay."

"You know I've been trying to write her," he continued. "She returns all of my mail. How can she still be so mad all these years later?"

"I don't know, Daddy," Dionne responded. "She doesn't talk to me about it." I sat in silence, taking in the conversation between father and daughter as I tried not to focus on my phobia. I noticed as Jermaine's eyes focused on me.

"And who is this?" he asked.

"Oh, I'm so rude," Dionne laughed. "Daddy, this is my best friend, Kamila. I've been telling you about her."

"Oh yes," he said, sitting back in his chair. "You're Sheila's little girl."

"Yes sir," I responded as Dionne passed me the phone.

"How is Sheila?" he asked, stroking his beard.

"She's doing okay," I said. "You know my mother?"

"Oh yes," he replied. "Sheila and I go a long way back. We all lived in the Greens back in the day."

"Oh cool," I said, preparing to give Dionne back the phone.

"Oh, don't go yet," Jermaine said. "What's your dad's name? I may know his people, too."

"Royal Sanders," I responded. He continued to stroke his beard, appearing to be in deep thought.

"How much do you know about Royal?" he asked.

"Not much since he passed away before I was born. Momma doesn't talk about him much and his family doesn't really have much to do with me." He paused for a moment as I looked over to Dionne, who seemed to be just as confused by his line of questioning as I was.

"I'm sorry to hear about that," he muttered. "Girl shouldn't have to grow up without knowing her daddy."

"It's okay," I responded. "I manage. As I'm sure Dionne manages your difficult situation. I'll give the phone back…"

"Wait!" he exclaimed. "How much do you know about my situation?"

"Not much," I shrugged. "I really don't ask."

"It's time I tell you. Both of you." He motioned for Dionne and the two of us put the phone between us so we could both hear. Knots began to form in my stomach as it appeared a man that I had just met knew more about me and my parents than I had ever been told. Momma was the type to say things like "none of your business" or "because I said so" if I asked too many questions.

"Dionne, baby," he began. "Do you know why I'm in here?"

"Yes, Daddy," Dionne replied. "You killed a man."

"Do you know the name of the man I killed?"

"No. It wasn't something that Momma talked much about."

"I'm sure she wouldn't have," he responded, looking down at his lap. "The truth is, 28 years ago, I killed a man.

And that man's name was Royal Sanders." I could feel the color flush from my face as his words registered in my mind. This man, the man Dionne had me drive for hours to see, was the man who took my father from me before I even had the opportunity to draw my first breath. He was the reason why I spent every Father's Day at Burr Oak Cemetery instead of in my father's arms. I wanted to scream. I wanted to tell him to go to hell, but all I could do was sit in silence as hot, steaming tears streamed down my face.

"Are you okay?" Dionne asked, touching my shoulder. "I know this is a lot to take in." I nodded. What choice did I have? I couldn't run screaming from the room. I could have, but it wouldn't have done any good.

"There's more," he said. *More?* My breaths grew heavy. *Was this why Momma freaked out when she heard I was coming here?*

"A long time ago, while I was married to Valerie, I had a little thing on the side with Sheila. It wasn't my proudest moment being that I was married and Sheila was still in high school but truthfully speaking, I loved Sheila. I would have done anything for her. But as much as I loved her, I loved Valerie and I had an obligation to her since she was carrying my seed. So I broke it off with Sheila and decided to stay with Valerie. I guess Sheila got to feeling guilty about everything because she told her boyfriend about us. He whooped her ass

97

and came looking for me. His intention was to kill me. It just happened to go the other way around."

"I think I've heard enough," I said, fighting the dry heaves in my throat. Not only did he kill my father, but his old ass was sleeping with my mother behind Dionne's mother's back. That explained why our mothers would never speak to each other.

"There's one more thing," he said. "Royal isn't your father. I am."

"Time's up!" the guard called, walking from the wall towards Jermaine. He glanced with sad eyes at Dionne and me as the two of us sat in complete shock. Although I didn't know what she was thinking, I knew we were both flooded with thoughts. *Was this man my father? Was Dionne my real life sister?*

***

There was an eerie silence during the ride back to the city. Dionne stared out of the passenger side window as I got lost in Musiq Soulchild's *Aijuswanasing* album. I just wanted to pretend the day never happened but there was no way I could. I wanted to think Jermaine was lying but Momma definitely had something to hide if she didn't want me to meet him.

"How do you feel?" Dionne asked as I neared her apartment.

"I don't know," I responded. "This is too much. You?"

"I'm in shock. You gotta know I didn't know any of this. I wouldn't have asked you to take me if…"

"Don't worry, Dee," I replied. "I don't blame you. The truth was going to come out eventually. Besides, this had to be a lot for you too."

"It is," Dionne said. "I definitely have some questions for my momma."

Oh please believe, I had questions for mine too.

Chapter Ten

My eyes burned. My body was heavy like weights after sinking to the bottom of an ocean. I didn't sleep much the night before and had been driving all day with Dionne so my initial plan was to go home and get some much-needed rest. But sleeping was the last thing I could do. I still didn't know what I was going to do about Demarcus or Jesse, but I had bigger fish to fry. The man I called Daddy, the man I mourned and cried for as I kneeled at his grave site could have possibly not been my daddy after all. This stranger I just met in prison, Dionne's daddy could have been my daddy. Dionne could have been my sister. So many questions swam through my mind as I drove aimlessly around the city. After dropping Dionne off, I drove south. I knew where I wanted to go and who I wanted to talk to, but I was hesitant. My mother and I did not have heart to heart conversations. We had grown from a parent-child relationship of her telling me to shut up because she told me so to a parent-adult child relationship of anger and unspoken resentment. I didn't want to be that way with her. Big Momma had always told me Sheila would be the only mother I would ever have and as resistant to that theory as I was when I was a child, Big Momma was right. And since Big Momma was no longer with us, I no longer her as a buffer. It was just me and Momma, and I was sure this conversation would be ugly. I was angry and hurt and I knew she was already against me going to the prison in the first place. Now I knew why.

After driving past the family building, I finally got the nerve to turn back so I could face my mother. It was 11:30 pm, but it was Saturday night and I was sure Momma would be awake. I parked the car and walked up the stairs to her apartment. I watched my breaths, making sure to contain my anger. I could hear Big Momma's voice in my mind saying, "Okay, lil girl. She's still your momma." Funny thing was, she never really acted like a mother to me. If anything, I felt like I filled the role when Big Momma was no longer around to keep Momma away from the liquor store.

Momma stared me down as she opened her apartment door. Her natural brown hair was tied in a pink bandana. She wore a pink and white striped nightgown with fuzzy pink slippers. She pursed her lips, placing one hand on her hip.

"If you're here for dinner, you're a bit late," she hissed. "I didn't put you up a plate because you should have been here."

I counted to ten inside my mind before I spoke. "I had something to do. I'm sure you knew that though." I invited myself inside as I knew she wasn't going to.

"So how was your trip?" she asked, following me into the living room. I sat on the couch and looked at her. She had her typical defensive stance, but something in her eyes seemed different and unfamiliar. I couldn't quite put my finger on it.

"It was informative," I responded, leaning forward and placing a hand under my chin. "Jermaine had a great deal to say to me."

Momma sighed and grabbed the sides of her heads in frustration. "This is why I didn't want you to go," she breathed.

"No, you didn't want me to find out."

"I wanted you to know, Kamila," she snapped. "Just in my own way."

"Your own way? This is my life, Momma!"

"I know that!"

"Do you?" Any façade of calm I had started to disappear.

"Yes, I know, Kamila. It wasn't just your life. Many lives were affected by this, including mine."

"I don't know if you know this, Momma, but life isn't always just about you." She looked at me in disbelief as she took a step backward.

"Who are you talking to?" she asked.

"I'm talking to you." She stepped closer and I could hear quickening in her breath. I knew she was angry. Maybe she felt I was being disrespectful to her but right then, I didn't care. I came for answers and I wasn't leaving until I got them.

As we stared each other down, I heard heavy footsteps on the hallway staircase. The door flung open as Silas rushed in, forcing his way between us.

"Hey, hey!" he shouted. "What's going on? Fighters to your corners!" I took a deep breath as I took a few steps back. Momma looked bewildered as she pressed her body against Silas' outstretched hand.

"Does he know?" I asked Momma.

"Shut up, Kamila," she hissed.

"Does he know?"

"I'm warning you!"

"Know what?" he asked.

"I found out why she didn't want me to take Dionne to see her dad."

"Kamila," Momma hissed through gritted teeth.

"The secrets out, Momma," I cried. "All the threatening and hushing you do won't stop that." She lowered her head, looking a bit defeated as Silas focused his eyes on me.

"What secret?" he asked.

"I took Dionne to visit her dad in prison. I didn't plan on going inside but she insisted. She wanted me to meet her dad."

"Little bitch probably did it on purpose," Momma muttered.

"Sheila!" Silas fussed. He turned his attention back to me. "Go on, baby girl."

"Dionne wanted me to meet her dad. They talked for a bit and he started asking me questions about the family... specifically Momma and my dad. I told him my father died before I was born. He told me he was in prison for killing my dad."

"Now that is true," Silas said. "And I'm sorry you had to find out that way."

"You knew?" I cried.

104

He nodded. "It wasn't my place to tell you."

I collapsed onto the couch. I couldn't get too upset with Silas because he was right. It wasn't his place to tell me. It was Momma's.

"But there's more," I said. Momma started hyperventilating as she sat down on the chair across from me.

"I don't want to hear it," she whispered.

"But…"

"I said I don't want to hear it, Kamila," she yelled.

"Sheila," Silas interjected. "This has gone on long enough. She's 27 years old. This conversation has to happen." He turned to me. "Go on, baby."

"Jermaine said the reason why he killed my dad was that my dad found out Jermaine and Momma were messing around. He beat Momma up and went after Jermaine with a gun. My dad intended on killing Jermaine but Jermaine ended up killing my dad instead."

Silas paused. His eyes grew large as he looked towards Momma. He looked back at me. "Now he's probably lying about that," he said, shaking his head.

I looked at Momma. It appeared as though the truth of my words escaped my mouth and ran down her throat, stealing her oxygen. It was then I knew for sure Jermaine wasn't lying. He was telling the truth.

"Sheila?" Silas asked, looking at my mother. "She's wrong, right? You weren't messing with that older, *married* man, were you?"

Momma sat still with her lips slightly parted, not saying a word.

"Sheila!" he shouted. Still, she sat silent.

"He also says that Royal isn't my dad. He says he's my dad."

"I don't have to listen to this," Momma said, standing up from the chair. Silas stepped back, cutting her off in her tracks.

"Sit down, Sheila," he commanded.

"Silas, you're not my daddy," she protested.

"I said sit down!" Momma stomped like a kindergartener in trouble, taking a seat back in the chair. For a moment, she glared at me with pure resentment, but then let out a relenting sigh.

"I guess I can't hold on to this forever," she sighed, looking off into the distance. Silas sat down next to me and held my hand. "Royal was my high school sweetheart and the love of my life. He was just starting to get into the game and was able to do things for me Momma couldn't and I loved him. But one day when I was standing at the bus stop, Jermaine pulled up and spoke to me. The man had a car! I'm not proud of it, but it felt good that he looked at me and didn't see a little high school girl."

"But you were a little high school girl," Silas interrupted.

"Silas," Momma sighed.

"I'm sorry," he said, holding up his hands. "Go ahead."

"I didn't intend on doing anything with Jermaine initially. I kept his phone number, except I didn't plan on calling him, but Royal started getting the big head. He was talking to other girls around school and just being an asshole so when I ran into Jermaine the second time, I let him give me a ride and we ended up going to his place - or what I thought was his place. We went to his homeboy's place for a while. Once I found out that it wasn't his place and confronted him, that's when I found out about Valerie. I stopped dealing with him for a while and by then, Royal and I had worked things out but Jermaine still wanted to be with me and he could do things for me that Royal couldn't, so we kept dealing with each other. But once I got pregnant with you, that's when everything changed. I couldn't keep going back and forth between two men and it made sense that Royal should be your dad because he was my age and wasn't married. I didn't want to cause Jermaine or myself any unnecessary problems.

So I broke it off with Jermaine. I didn't even tell him I was pregnant. I don't know how he could know you're his daughter. But I did end up coming clean to Royal about sleeping with Jermaine and the possibility of him not being your father. He went off. And he did slap me, but I kind of had it coming. And he went after Jermaine. I knew what I did was wrong but I didn't know that it would blow up the way it did and ruin so many lives. I was just young and stupid and having fun." Tears started to stream down her face. Outside of Big Momma's funeral, this was the only time I ever saw my mother cry.

I sat in silence, looking at my mother and uncle. I tried to take in everything she was saying to me. Could that be the reason why she was so adamant about me reconciling with Jesse and not because of his money or who his family was? I had so many questions. I still wanted to be angry with her, but right then, all I could see was a teenage girl with the world on her shoulders. I always imagined it would be difficult being a young girl with a baby in the womb. The stories of my conception served as birth control for me for many years. But not only was she a pregnant teen, her actions led to the death of a teenage boy and the incarceration of a married man. She took a man away from his pregnant wife and unborn daughter.

Suddenly, I went from feeling inconvenienced by Dionne and her father – *our* father, to feeling the need to apologize to Dionne and Valerie on behalf of my family. That was the reason why Momma and Valerie never spoke and now that I knew the truth, I couldn't blame Valerie. I started to wonder if she knew the truth about me. If so, it must have been hard for her spending all those days watching as I played with her daughter.

"I carried this secret for years," Momma muttered. "I would have taken it to my grave. I understand this is your life, Kamila, but there is more to this than you and me. Much more." She got up from the chair and walked off to bed, leaving me and Silas sitting on the couch.

"You okay, baby girl?" he asked.

"I don't know what I am anymore," I responded.

"Come on," he said, standing up from the couch. "You can stay at my place for the night. I don't want you driving home this late or in this state of mind."

I nodded as I followed him up the stairs.

Chapter Eleven - Dionne

Dionne's mind wandered as she walked up the steps to her apartment. When the day began, she was excited about the person she had considered her lifelong best friend meeting her father. It didn't hurt that Kamila had a car and a valid license since Dionne's lead foot along with her smart mouth caused her to not be able to drive for six months. She had plans for the remainder of the night but all of Dionne's focus was on the mind-boggling news she had just received from her father. She knew her mother had to have known, but Valerie never said a word to her about Kamila, Sheila, or Jermaine. In fact, aside from the generic acknowledgment of Jermaine being her father, Valerie rarely spoke of him at all. She wouldn't accept his calls or return his letters but Dionne would always assume her mother was simply angry with her father for doing something stupid, resulting in Valerie being a struggling single mother. Valerie never wanted to be a statistic and always taught Dionne that if she simply couldn't wait for marriage to have sex, she should at least be married before pushing out a baby because being a single mother was not as glamorous as so many women would make it seem. As a child, Dionne knew that Valerie would have nothing to worry about in that regard, but now that she knew the truth, she had a much deeper understanding of her mother's anger.

Dionne entered her apartment and flopped her exhausted body onto her bed. She knew her mother would probably be asleep because it was after 10 pm but she simply had to talk to her. She pulled out her cell phone to call her mother. Fatigue dripped from Valerie's voice as she answered the phone.

"Hello?"

"Hey Ma," Dionne smiled.

"Hey, baby girl! You made it back safe, I see."

"Yes, Kamila drove me."

"She did?" Valerie asked.

"Yes, I begged her. I even had her come in and meet him."

"I see," Valerie's voice became more alert and hesitant.

"He told her… us… everything."

"I knew it would come out eventually," Valerie said.

"Why didn't you ever tell me?"

"I was angry. I didn't marry that man for him to sleep around with some high school girl. He threw his life away along with our marriage and any opportunity to be a real father in your life."

Dionne's chest felt weighted as she took in her mother's words.

"I guess I could understand but did you know that Kamila was his daughter?"

"I knew it was a possibility. I knew he was messing with that little girl. The wife always knows. Truthfully, Kamila's grandmother knew it was a possibility as well. That's why she always wanted to make sure you and Kamila had each other. It took a bit for me to warm up to the idea, personally. I wanted nothing to do with the little girl that destroyed my family but Mary was right. Ultimately, Kamila was the blessing in all of this. She lost a father in this whole mess before she was even born and you were born not too long after all of this happened. If nothing else, it was nice that the two of you always had each other."

"I guess I wish I had known she was my sister all these years," Dionne muttered.

"But you two were always like sisters anyway, Dee."

"This is true."

"It wasn't the best of circumstances. I couldn't protect you from having to go in and out of those prisons as a child but I was happy you and Kamila had a sisterly bond even when you didn't know you were sisters. And you know how that mother of hers is so you're going to need to be her light in all of this darkness."

"Of course," Dionne smiled. She always tried to be the peace in Kamila's life, but she took on more of a role when Mary passed away. Now that things were rocky with Jesse, she knew that her friend – her sister – would need her more than ever.

As Dionne continued talking to her mother, she could hear a knock on her front door. She felt goosebumps as she grinned with excitement.

"Ma, I gotta go," she smiled.

"I'll be glad when you get over this little phase and settle down somewhere," Valerie groaned.

"It's not a phase, Ma. I love you too."

"If you really loved me…"

"Bye Ma!" Dionne ended the call and rushed from her bedroom to open the front door. *Maybe the night can be salvaged,* she thought to herself.

The hallway light beamed from Adriana's chocolate-colored skin as she stood in the doorway. She flashed a bright smile from her plump burgundy lips as she entered the apartment, greeting Dionne with a hug.

"Hey Babe," Adriana smiled, kissing Dionne on her flushed cheek. "How was the trip?"

"Eye-opening," Dionne responded as she intertwined her fingers with Adriana's, guiding her into the living room."

"Oh?"

"Yes. I found out today that Kamila and I are actual blood sisters."

Adriana raised a manicured eyebrow as she sat on the couch next to Dionne. "Well, you said you two were always like sisters, right?"

"Sure," Dionne shrugged. "There were a lot of times I wished she was my real life sister but I would have never imagined she'd become my sister this way. It turns out my dad had an affair with her mom while her mom was still in high school. Sheila's boyfriend found out and went to confront my dad. Sheila's boyfriend is the reason why my dad has been in prison my entire life."

Adriana sank back into the couch. Her eyes bulged in disbelief as she breathed an exhausted sigh.

"That's a lot to take in," she said.

"I know." Dionne fell back, resting her head on Adriana's breasts. "It was a whole lot. I wasn't able to take it all in because it pretty much destroyed Kamila's world once she got the news. She lived her entire life thinking Royal was her dad and as it turns out, her real father was the man who killed him. I mean… my dad was running around on my mom with an underage girl. I've spent years of my life traveling on Greyhound buses with my mom to visit him in prison. I'm trying not to judge and I know everyone makes mistakes but…"

"You have a right to feel, Dee," Adriana interrupted, as she placed her fingers under Dionne's chin, lifting it so Dionne could see into her eyes. "I know this must suck for Kamila but it doesn't mean it can't suck for you too."

"I know," Dionne whispered. She looked into the sparkling amber of Adriana's eyes. "And I called my mom to talk to her about it. She was pretty helpful until she heard you at the door."

"It will be all right," Adriana responded.

"She said she'd be happy once I'm through this phase. I love my mom and all but I hate when she does that."

"She loves you. And hell, at least she still talks to you."

"Still no word from Camryn, huh?"

"No," Adriana nodded. "The girl gives herself a pass for having four kids out of wedlock with three different men but having a sister who's a lesbian is a deal breaker for some reason."

"Cherry-picking the Bible," Dionne responded. "It's something so many people do. I still haven't told Mila about us and she's been asking if I had someone in my life."

"What's stopping you?"

"I don't know how she'll react. I don't think she's a homophobe but I still have to deal with my mom and the people from my mom's church and I couldn't take Kamila treating me differently or like how your sister treats you."

"You gotta give her a chance," Adriana said. "She might surprise you. Besides, I wouldn't mind meeting her. She seems like an important part of your life."

"You are too," Dionne replied, leaning in for a kiss. They traded deep, passionate kisses as Adriana wrapped her arms around Dionne. She leaned back onto the couch, pulling Dionne on top of her. Dionne cupped Adriana's breasts while

Adriana lifted Dionne's skirt. Dionne straddled Adriana as Adriana shifted Dionne's panties to the side, rubbing and caressing her before sliding two fingers inside her essence. Dionne moaned deeply while grinding herself onto Adriana's fingers. They continued trading kisses as Dionne pulled down Adriana's white tank top, pulling her breasts out of her shirt. Dionne shifted down Adriana's body, placing a nipple into her mouth. Adriana's chest rose into Dionne's kisses as she rubbed her hands through Dionne's curly hair. Dionne pulled herself from Adriana's embrace, standing before her as she pulled down Adriana's pants. Adriana gazed at Dionne from the couch with wanting as Dionne kneeled before her, licking her lips before teasing Adriana's womanhood with kisses and licks. Adriana moaned as her hips rocked, welcoming Dionne's tongue. Her body became flushed as she gripped Dionne's hair, shoving her face deep inside of her. Dionne could feel shakes coming from Adriana's legs as she doubled down, pushing her tongue deeper into Adriana. Adriana moaned and cried softly as she poured her nectar into Dionne's waiting mouth. She sat up, pulling Dionne's face to hers and giving her deep kisses.

"My turn," Adriana whispered. She pulled down Dionne's skirt and panties before directing her onto the couch, placing her on her stomach. Adriana pulled Dionne up by the hips, hoisting her behind into the air. Adriana crawled behind Dionne on the couch, shoving her tongue into Dionne

117

as moisture covered Dionne's inner thighs. Dionne moaned loudly as she moved her hips up and down. Adriana gripped Dionne's thighs, pulling her close as she flicked her tongue around. Dionne's moans turned into stuttered mutterings of Adriana's name mixed with a few expletives before collapsing from her position on her knees on the couch. Adriana laid on top of Dionne, kissing her ears and the back of her neck.

"I love you," she whispered.

"I love you too," Dionne replied.

Chapter Twelve

Silas took the couch, letting me sleep on his king-sized bed. The mattress felt so soft under my skin that I could almost ignore the man funk mixed with the scent of his Newport cigarettes. Before I went to bed, I called Jesse to let him know I'd be staying over so he wouldn't worry. The most recent days of our relationship had been spent with me avoiding him because of his tryst with Cassandra, and then there was my own incident with Demarcus, but at that moment, I just wanted to collapse into his arms and feel just a little bit of normal. I had yet to have the chance to fill him in on my trip to the prison or my emotionally exhausting conversation with my mother. As comforted as I felt being with Silas, I needed a sort comfort that my uncle couldn't provide to me.

I could hear the sound of Silas' loud snoring coming from the living room as I reached over to my purse for my cell phone. I had a missed call from Jesse. I called him back.

"How'd you sleep?" he asked.

"As well as I could under the circumstances."

"Oh?"

"Babe, I learned a lot from my visit to the prison. It turned out to be more for me than it was for Dionne. It turns out that Dionne and I are half-sisters."

"Really?" he asked.

"Yes and there's so much more to it than that. It was a lot, Jesse."

"Well, I'm sure we can talk about all of that once you're home," he responded dryly. I wasn't even sure if he was listening to me.

"I guess," I said. I didn't have the emotional strength to protest his insensitivity.

"I need you home tonight, Kamila," he continued. "Mother is having a dinner tonight for the entire family and I'd like you to be there."

"Jesse, I'm not really in the condition to have dinner with your family," I sighed. The pure truth was the Bennetts —

specifically, the female Bennetts– did not care for me. The feeling was pretty mutual. Jesse's mother and sister were a special type of saddidy that one gets when one has had money for a long time and forgets that one is black. His mother Carolyn came from very meager beginnings in rural Mississippi and shared a bedroom with four sisters. She changed her name from Myrtle Jean to Carolyn once she moved north. The only reason I knew this information was because Jesse's father exposed her one night after becoming annoyed with one of her self-righteous taunts of me.

"Kamila, please," Jesse pleaded.

"I guess," I sighed.

"I love you."

"Yeah," I replied, returning his dryness. "Me too." I ended the call.

I went downstairs to Big Momma's apartment to grab a quick shower so I could leave. I was sure that Silas wouldn't have cared for me leaving without saying goodbye but right then, I really didn't feel like speaking to anyone - especially my mother. I grabbed the tunic dress from the closet, quickly got dressed and ran for the door. I stepped outside to find Janette leaning on the hood of my car.

"Good morning, Mimi," she said with a mischievous smile. "You weren't going to leave without saying goodbye, were you?"

"Considering the fact that I'd never actually say hello to you," I responded. "I'm not in the mood, Janette. What do you want?"

"I'm sorry to inconvenience you," she said as she stood up from my car. She waved her hands as she spoke, holding a cell phone in one of them. "I just wanted to show you something I'm sure you'd want to see."

"I doubt it," I responded.

"You sure? I don't know if you knew I took up a little hobby recently."

"I don't care, Janette," I snapped. She was beginning to piss me off.

"Oh, but you'll care about this. See, I was taking a walk outside the other night and I got some pretty interesting shots."

I rolled my eyes. She wasn't going to leave me alone until I either cracked her jaw or looked at the pictures. Looking at the pictures would probably have been easier than explaining to Jesse why we both had to miss his parents' dinner due to my needing representation.

"Show me the fucking pictures," I groaned.

She smiled and clapped with excitement. "Oh good, you have time!" she squealed as she pulled up the pictures in her phone before proudly holding it to my face. It was me and Demarcus, engaged in full lip lock as the strange man looked on. I could feel a bit of color flush from my face.

"You know," she continued. "You outta be careful of your surroundings when you're kissing somebody who isn't your boyfriend."

"What's your point?" I asked, attempting to regain my composure. I wasn't exactly worried about what she'd do with the pictures. She had never even met Jesse and I doubted she knew how to contact him but I was sloppy. I made out with my ex-boyfriend on a public street where anyone could have seen us and someone, in fact, saw us. Not just someone, but Janette. Not only did I knock myself off my soapbox, but I did it unknowingly in front of the worst possible person.

"I don't have much of a point," she smiled. "But wait, I do. You're no better than I am."

"On my worse day, I'll still be better than you," I responded, feigning confidence.

"Oh, I don't think so. Janette the hoe. That's what you and your homegirl call me and yet here you are, locking lips with a man who ain't yours. I find this very interesting."

123

"Let's not forget he isn't mine because of you, Janette. We're not the same."

"I wonder if lawyer boy would agree," she responded.

"Who's to say what he will believe," I replied, shrugging my shoulders. "That's for me to find out. At either rate, it's none of your business."

"Maybe not," she smiled. "But I'd like to think that the contents of my phone are my business and you never know when my path will cross his."

"I'm not worried about that," I growled, stepping closer to Janette. She was pissing me off for multiple reasons and the more she spoke, the less I was concerned about cracking that jaw. "Jesse doesn't work cases of prostitution. Now if you excuse me, I have somewhere to be. Unless you want me to remove you from my vehicle."

She smirked as she walked around me, away from the car. "See you next time, Mimi."

I got in the car and sped off without a response.

***

A chilly air swept through the Bennett home as Jesse and I stepped inside. I purposely chose to wear the tunic dress I wore at the club, hoping he would notice my bare legs and possibly comment on them.

"You look nice," He said. That was it. He wasn't concerned about my trip to the prison, my parents, or the fight I had with my mother. In fact, he didn't ask about me at all.

"Father's having some important clients over for dinner so I'm going to need my girl to bring that Future Mrs. Bennett charm." That was it. He wanted me to be his arm candy and pretend that Jesse and I were the Urban Cinderella and Prince Charming we were before everything went to hell.

Jesse took my jacket and hung it in the hall closet as I stood in the foyer, looking around at the walls of mirror and gold statues that lined the hall. Although I had been to his parents' house several times, I still felt like an awkward visitor every time I was there, much to Jesse's chagrin. He wanted me to get along with his family and it wasn't that I didn't want to, but they made it uncomfortable at every turn.

"Please try," he whispered, guiding me into the dining room.

"Jesse!" Hannah called as she ran from the kitchen, jumping into her brother's arms. Her pale cheeks flushed with happiness as her platinum blond weave danced across the air. My face immediately felt hot as I stepped away from the two of them.

"Hey kiddo," he smiled. "How are things?"

"Outside of finals kicking my tail, pretty well!"

Jesse gave me an expectant look. I was sure he wanted me to say hello to Hannah. There were many things I wanted to say to her but hello was not one of them.

"Hello, Kamila," she smiled. I nodded.

"Kamila," Jesse insisted.

"Hi Hannah," I responded.

"And how are you?" she asked.

"I'm quite well considering."

"Considering?"

"Considering your last visit to our place with your little friend."

"Kamila!" Jesse exclaimed. "Not now!" I shrugged.

"Oh, you mean Cassandra!" Hannah exclaimed. "She would have been here but she was concerned for her safety. She wanted me to tell you hi, Jess."

I clutched my fist as I stepped towards her. I could see the heat radiating from Jesse's face as he treaded between us.

"Girls," he cried. "You have to stop this! Tonight is too important to Father."

"I told you I was in no condition to come!" I snapped, as I turned towards the front door.

"You can take the rat out of the hood," she sang. That was it. I spun around, punching Hannah square in the jaw. She stumbled and fell to the floor. That one punch contained all of my rage. The rage for my mother, for Jesse, for Janette, for Cassandra, for Hannah, and for myself. At that moment, I was pushed to the brink and could care less about Jesse's image or his family.

"She should be arrested!" Hannah cried from the floor. Jesse rushed to her side.

"Fuck all of you," I snarled as I ran from the house.

I walked half a mile from the Bennetts' house to 95th and Kedzie. We drove to the house in Jesse's car so I had no transportation. I fished around in my purse for bus fare as my cell phone vibrated with incessant calls from Jesse. I didn't want to talk to him. I hadn't talked to Dionne since dropping her off and now wasn't the time. I couldn't talk to Silas without risking crossing paths with my mother. There was only one person I could think of at that moment. Perhaps I was losing my mind but right then, I needed him. Demarcus.

Chapter Thirteen

Demarcus's white Crown Victoria pulled up to the bus stop where I sat. He opened the passenger side door from the driver's seat, wearing a black wife beater, black doo-rag, and jeans. I quickly wiped tears from my face as I stood from the bench, taking a seat on the passenger's side and closing the door.

"Thank you for coming to get me," I said.

"I'm actually glad you called me," Demarcus smiled. "We hadn't spoken since that night."

"I know," I responded. "I needed time to think."

"Did you have time to think?"

"No." My attempt to hide my emotions failed as tears escaped my eyes like water from a broken dam. Demarcus rubbed my shoulder as he looked at me with concern. This was the concern I sought from Jesse. The concern I sought from my mother.

"Let me get you away from here," he said.

As we drove down Kedzie, the tears continued to pour as I gave Demarcus every detail of events since I last saw him. I told him of the trip to the prison, the ugly confrontation with my mother, and the even uglier confrontation with Jesse and his sister. He listened to my every rambling without seeking ways to turn the attention to himself as Momma and Jesse had usually done. He just let me have my moment.

"Oh," I said. "Can we not go to your mom's place? I forgot to tell you Janette took a picture of us kissing and made sure I knew she had it."

"That girl," Demarcus sighed. "I know where we can go." He made a right on 87th and drove east to an area I wasn't very familiar with. As he drove, my body began to feel the effects of the past few days. I fought the tiredness I felt as I wanted to be aware of my surroundings. I could feel the vibrations from my cell phone in my pocket as my eyelids fluttered open and closed. Suddenly, I couldn't fight anymore.

***

When I opened my eyes, I found myself in a dimly-lit bedroom. I was tucked in bed, fully clothed aside from my shoes. As I got up from the bed and walked into the hallway, I could hear Demarcus's voice along with another male voice. It sounded like they were playing NBA 2K18 and trash talking each other. I walked into the living room to see Demarcus and the man seated on the couch, engaged in their video game. The stranger caught sight of me first before nudging Demarcus.

"Hey sleepy head," Demarcus smiled. "You hungry?"

"Where am I?" I asked, rubbing my eyes.

"It seemed like you could use some rest, so I brought you to my cousin's house. This is her fiancé, Will."

Will stood from the couch and extended his hand. "Pleasure, Ma'am."

"Nice to meet you," I smiled, shaking his hand.

"My cousin, Nadia is in the kitchen fixing some dinner," Demarcus said. "You hungry?"

"I'm starved," I responded. "But I probably shouldn't stay too long."

A thin, butterscotch-colored woman emerged from the kitchen carrying two plates of burritos and rice. She gave one plate to Demarcus and the other to Will.

"Hey girl!" she exclaimed, hugging me as if we were lifelong friends. "I thought you would never wake up! I was about to call 911 or something. You hungry?"

"Yes," I laughed.

"Come on into the kitchen," Nadia smiled. "It's too much testosterone in here."

"Go make me a sammich, woman!" Will laughed, as he gave his fiancée's behind a playful slap.

I followed Nadia into the kitchen. Her long brown hair was pulled back into a braid that swayed back and forth along with her hips. She motioned for me to take a seat at the kitchen table while she fixed my plate.

"Girl, I have heard so much about you," she said. "I swear you're the only girl Demarcus has ever loved."

"Really?" My stomach tightened with nervousness, but I was a bit delighted to know that he still thought of me in that regard.

"Yes! You think he would go out and carry any other woman up in here?"

"I don't know," I responded. "Demarcus and I hadn't really been in touch for quite some time. Things kind of went sour when we were kids and I'm in a relationship right now."

"Blah, blah, blah," Nadia laughed. "Y'all were kids. I know about all of that. But you're here right now, aren't you?"

"Well, yes."

She placed the plate in front of me and I took a bite. Nadia was a pretty good cook. Before I knew it, my plate was completely empty. I guess in all the commotion, I hadn't eaten very much.

"Thank you for the meal," I said, standing from my seat. "I really should be leaving."

"Girl," Nadia laughed. "Where are you gonna go? From what Demarcus tells me, going home right now may not be the best idea and do you really want to go to your mother's?" She was right. Normally, I'd run home to the comfort of Big Momma's apartment or I'd spend time with Silas. Neither of those seemed to appeal to me.

"You can stay here for the night until things calm down," Nadia smiled.

"I'll be okay," I insisted. "But thank you."

"Okay, girl," she shrugged.

I walked back into the living room where the men had switched from playing virtual basketball to watching a live game.

"Demarcus," I said. "I think I should be going."

"Yeah, okay," he said, standing from his seat.

I went back to the bedroom where I slept to collect my shoes and purse. I pulled out my cell phone to check my messages.

Jesse: Kamila, answer the phone! I don't know where you are, who you're with or if you're okay. You hit my sister and then run out of here like some sort of mad woman. Thankfully, she's not pressing charges.

Jesse: Kamila... look... please answer the phone. Let's talk about this. Help me see where you're coming from because I don't understand.

Jesse: Kamila, I'll be home tonight if you wish to talk. We're better than this. Please.

Momma: Kamila, this is your mother. Call me.

Dionne: Um, Bitch, I know you don't call yourself avoiding me now that we're sisters and all. You'd better call me!

I was relieved to hear Dionne's voice within all of that craziness. I quickly dialed her number.

"Bitch, I was about to send the dogs out," Dionne laughed.

"No need," I responded. "I'm here."

"What you doing tonight?"

"Having a sleepover with you if that's cool."

"Aw hell, what you done got into now?" she asked.

"It's a long story," I responded. "I'll fill you in once I'm there."

Demarcus and I left Nadia's apartment and got back into his car.

"What you think Dionne's gonna say when you pull up with me?" he asked.

"What won't she say?" I laughed. "That's the last thing I'm worried about right now." We paused and stared into each other's eyes. It was as if the last ten years had never happened. It felt like we were still those kids without a care in the world.

"When did it happen?" I sighed.

"What?"

"When did we grow up?"

"Hell," Demarcus laughed. "I don't know. I wish I had a say in it."

"You and me both," I smiled.

"What are we doing, Mila?"

"What do you mean?" I asked.

"I mean, I'm glad you called me but why did you call me? Why did you sleep with me and then run away from me? What are we doing here?"

"I don't know," I muttered. The questions he asked had been going through my mind since the first night I ran into him at Exodus.

"I think that's something we need to figure out."

"We?"

"Yes," he responded. "We. Kamila, you broke up with me because I made a mistake. Granted, it was a stupid mistake, but it was one mistake. You completely cut me off. And yet, here you are pushing me away for a clown who I'm sure has done way more than one stupid teenage mistake." He was right.

"I broke up with you because you and I were in a relationship and you broke the rules of that relationship."

"Rules… black and white. You've always been very black and white, Kamila. How is that working out for you?"

"What does that mean?" I crossed my arms and turned to him as my eyes narrowed.

"It means you broke up with me because I broke the rules by sleeping with Janette. By that logic, Jesse should break up with you, right?"

135

"Technically yes, and by that same logic, I should have broken up with him first."

"So he cheated on you?"

"Yes."

I looked into his face as he focused on the road. I could see small traces of a tear form in the corner of his eye.

"He cheated on you. He broke the same rule I broke but he still has a fighting chance."

"We're not kids anymore, Demarcus. Life isn't simple."

"Life is as hard as you make it, Kamila. I still love you. I've been Public Enemy Number One for a mistake that I've spent years of my life regretting and you're still committed to this dude who probably doesn't even love the real you."

"That's not fair, Demarcus," I said as my own tears started to form.

"The truth ain't always fair, baby," he shrugged. "And the truth is I still love you. And I can tell you still love me. This thing was never finished. It was just thrown on pause. You can stay with this Jesse cat. You can marry him and have ten of his babies but you'll know in your mind that you and I were never finished."

Hot, stinging tears began to fall down my face. He was right. I ended our relationship after catching him with Janette, something he had done when he was seventeen years old and I didn't give the decision much thought. I carried myself with an air of moral superiority for years because of what he did to me. Although I took Jesse back after being with Cassandra, I had been a total nightmare to him. I told myself I would never be the hot mess I felt my mother was but as I sat in Demarcus's car, I realized that I was no better or worse than either of these people. We were all flawed people who had done things to hurt others and it was high time for me to forgive all of them as well as myself.

"I'm not sure what we're doing, Demarcus," I whimpered. "In time, we will figure this out. I'd like to try and work things out with Jesse, but you're right. We do have some things to work out between us."

"I can respect that," he responded.

Demarcus parked the car in front of Dionne's apartment building. Dionne stood on the front porch smoking a cigarette, which she tossed once her eyes met ours.

"Aw hell no!" she shouted, stomping down the stairs. "Cruz, what the hell are you doing over here?"

"Umm…" Demarcus stumbled over his words while looking to me for help.

"And she's crying?" Dionne exclaimed. "Oh, I'm gonna have to cut you! Get out the car, Cruz!"

I wiped my face and hopped out of the car. "It's not his fault, Dee."

Dionne took a step back and let out a loud sigh. "She saved your life, dude," she said.

"I'll talk to y'all later," Demarcus called. I waved goodbye as Dionne nodded. Demarcus sat and watched while the two of us walked inside before pulling off into the night.

Chapter Fourteen

"Okay girl, start talking," Dionne commanded as we entered her apartment. The scent of her last blunt still lingered in the air as Carl Thomas' *I Wish* played on her CD player. I dragged my exhausted body over to the living room and plopped down on the couch while Dionne stood over me, giving her best schoolmarm stance.

"Girl," I sighed. "It's been a rough few days."

"I know that much," she said, sitting down on the carpet to roll her next blunt. "How'd you end up in a car with Cruz?"

"Well, it started after confronting my mom over the information I got from your dad."

"Oh goodness. How did that go?"

"Oh, it was a disaster," I responded. "I knew it would be but after I dropped you off, I had to talk to her. I knew she was hiding something because she was dead set against me driving you to that prison."

"Yeah, I talked to my mom, too."

"How did that go?" I asked.

"Probably not as bad as your conversation went, but Mom knew all along it was a possibility you could have been my father's child. Apparently, she knew about your mom for a while before Royal found out. She told me, 'the wife always knows.' The word on the street was that they fought over some gang shit but my mom always knew what the real story was about. Your grandma might have known too. That was why your grandma and my mom always wanted to make sure we had each other growing up."

"It makes sense," I nodded. Big Momma was always about family. She used to say that family isn't always as neat and pretty as the old school sitcoms would make it out to be but in a pinch, family was all anyone ever had. It now made sense that Big Momma would sometimes take two city buses and a train to get Dionne whenever I wanted to have a sleepover or Valerie just needed a break. We always felt like we were sisters, not realizing we were real-life sisters all along.

"So how are you feeling about all of this?" Dionne asked, taking a hit from her blunt.

"Exhausted," I sighed. "The conversation with Momma got downright ugly. She was keeping this huge, ugly secret from me and I don't think Silas knew the full story either. He knew Jermaine killed Royal, but he never knew that Momma had a relationship with Jermaine. Silas was pretty disgusted considering the fact that Jermaine was a grown ass man at the time. No offense."

"None taken," Dionne laughed. "You have way more to be upset about than I do. Plus, I got my daily dose of Fukitol so nothing can piss me off right now." Dionne waved her Fukitol, otherwise known as her blunt, in the air. "You should try some with all the craziness you got going on."

"You know I can't," I responded, rolling my eyes.

"Oh yeah," Dionne replied. "Jesse. Well hell, it's not like you're giving a shit about what he wants if you're getting dropped off by Cruz. Let's not pretend we don't need to discuss that, by the way."

"I didn't forget," I groaned. "I'm getting to it. So after the heated discussion with Momma, Silas insisted I stay at his place because he didn't want me to drive. I called Jesse that morning looking for some sort of understanding, but all he was concerned about was his parents and their fancy dinner.

So I just went along with him. I even wore the dress I bought from Nordstrom and he didn't even notice."

"That's why you went and hopped on Cruz?" Dionne interrupted.

"Girl, let me get to it," I responded. "So anyways, we get to his parents' house, and his sister is talking crap. This is after Janette showed up at the house trying to blackmail me."

"No!" Dionne gasped. "Did you beat the breaks off her ass?"

"Not Janette."

"Hannah?" Dionne jumped to her feet in amazement. "You beat up his sister?"

"Girl, I wasn't even thinking about it. I begged Jesse not to pull me into his family's 'Let's put on airs' show that they like to do. I had already had a rough night but he was not concerned at all. I was mad at Momma, Jesse, Janette, myself - and Hannah said something about taking the rat out of the hood."

"No, she didn't!" Dionne exclaimed, stomping across the living room floor. The downstairs neighbor banged on his ceiling with a broomstick.

"Shut the fuck up, Roderick!" Dionne shouted towards the floor. "You don't hear me tripping when you be

142

having all of those hoes down there. Don't make me tell your wife!" The banging stopped.

"Now you," Dionne continued. "Hell, I probably would have clocked her ass too. But I know Jesse and his high-falluting ass family probably didn't care for you popping their pretty little princess like a balloon."

"I wouldn't know," I responded. "I basically cursed Jesse and his sister out and ran out of the house. Jesse drove so my car is at home. I walked to 95th and Kedzie and called Demarcus."

"Did y'all fuck again?"

"Actually, no. He took me to his cousin's house for some food and some rest and then he brought me here."

I thought back to my time at Nadia's house and the conversation with Demarcus on the way to Dionne's. She didn't need to know all of the details although I was sure she knew me well enough to know I still had some feelings for Demarcus. It was just nice to be able to be myself around Demarcus and his family. Nadia was willing to give me a place to stay whereas Hannah didn't think I was good enough to share her oxygen. My mind wandered around Demarcus's comments that Jesse didn't love the real me. Who else could he have been in love with for the last three years?

"So what about this blackmail?" Dionne asked, finishing up her blunt and snapping me back from my trance.

"Janette has pictures of Demarcus and me kissing," I shrugged.

"That little bitch," Dionne snarled as she shook her head. "Hoe thinks two plus two is twelve but give her somebody else's business and she becomes a genius."

"I'm not really worried about it," I said with a wave of my hand.

"She needs her ass beat," Dionne snapped.

"Well, I got my quota for the day." I wasn't sure why I was so dismissive about Janette's pictures. One click on any social media site could have had Demarcus and me on full blast for Jesse and the world to see, but I didn't care. Jesse didn't care about getting head in our living room, so why should I have cared? But at the same time, I couldn't help but wonder if there was something deeper going on. If I truly loved Jesse, I could have worked through this whole Cassandra mess, but over time, a fresh start with Demarcus had become more and more appealing.

Dionne and I sat up talking until sunrise. Thanks to the nap I caught at Nadia's, I didn't mind not getting any sleep. Calls from Jesse and Momma continued on my cell phone. I ignored them all, but there was one text message I simply could not ignore.

Demarcus: Just making sure you haven't gone postal on a brotha. Try and chill out some today.

Chapter Fifteen

I was able to pick up my car along with some clothes while Jesse was at work. I decided to stay with Dionne for a couple of days while I figured out my next move. After two or three days of ignoring him, I sent Jesse a text so he would know I was alive, well, and staying with Dionne. He was happy to know I was okay but insisted we needed to talk. I was not ready.

I was still not speaking to Momma but started to feel a bit bad for not dropping by the family building to spend time with Silas. He'd usually call and fuss at me by this point so it was a bit weird I hadn't heard from him. I decided I would go by and spend time with him after the much needed night out I had planned with Dionne.

I parked my car in front of Dionne's apartment and grabbed my suitcase from the trunk. I carried it up the steps and dragged it to Dionne's apartment and into her bedroom.

"How much did you bring?" she asked. "Don't be trying to bougie up my apartment with all of your saddidy shit!"

"Fuck you!" I laughed. I opened the suitcase and mulled over my options of what to wear to Exodus. I packed a deep purple pantsuit with a plunging neckline and strappy gold stilettos to match. I had silent hopes that we'd run into Demarcus at the club and he'd be able to take in all of my curves.

"Oh, I see you, bitch!" Dionne laughed as I pulled the pantsuit from my suitcase. "You trying to show out for Demarcus."

"I don't know what you're talking about," I lied.

"Sure you don't." Dionne pulled a white tank top and an ankle-length lavender skirt from her closet.

"How you even know he's gonna be there?" I asked.

"You and I both know he's gonna be there," Dionne sighed. "And the fact that you're fishing tells me you're hoping he will be there. Girl, you need to figure out what you're doing."

Although she and I both knew my true intentions, I couldn't admit that she was right. Here I was, pulling out all the stops for a man I swore I would never be with again while I was avoiding my current man like the plague. Outside of text messages here and there, I hadn't talked to Jesse since giving Hannah the much-deserved punch in the face. My fairytale love seemed to have become something from that old TV show, *The Outer Limits*. Jesse wasn't Jesse. I wasn't me. And Demarcus didn't appear to be that dirty cheating dog I cut off in high school. Life no longer made sense.

After a couple more hours of primping for Demarcus while lying to both Dionne and myself about my true intentions, we hopped in my car to get our night started. V103 played Freddie Jackson's *Jam Tonight*, taking me back to the days when Dionne and I were playing hopscotch in the projects while Big Momma yelled from the window for me to get my narrow ass up those steps.

"You think you might meet somebody tonight?" I asked.

"Heffa, how you know I don't have somebody already?" Dionne teased. "Just because you're bouncing between two bodies doesn't mean it's not enough out there for me."

"I never meet anybody you date, though. We're supposed to be girls… And damn! I'm your real life sister now so I gotta decide if I approve of the clown or not."

"I don't kiss and tell," Dionne replied, flipping her curls from her shoulders. This was one of those rare nights when she opted not to wear a head wrap.

"That's because you ain't kissing nobody with your dry bed having ass."

"Slut," Dionne laughed with a playful slap on my arm.

"Heffa, I'm driving. I will kill us both!"

We parked at the club and walked inside. It seemed we had just missed an awesome performance as the crowd was going crazy for this a bald brother while he took his final bow. For some odd reason, the dude opted to wear a black turtleneck with a white scarf around his neck in this humid weather. I thought he might have watched too many yuppie TV shows and was trying way too hard. As I watched this strange brother leave the stage, my eyes were covered by someone's hands. The smell of his cologne stirred everything within me that made me a woman. Demarcus.

"Guess who?" he whispered.

"Y'all need a motel room," Dionne fussed.

Demarcus moved his hands from my eyes and took the empty seat next to me.

"I was hoping to run into you two," he said.

"Us two?" Dionne laughed. "Okay, you two need to stop all that damn lying. I'm going to get a drink." Dionne got up and walked through the crowd towards the bar, leaving me with Demarcus.

"So you were hoping you'd see me?" I smiled.

"Of course," he responded. "I've been worried about you since I last saw you."

"I've been okay. I've just been taking my time, crashing at Dionne's."

"And you still have your hearing?" Demarcus teased.

"Partially. I have an appointment with an ear doctor in the morning." We both laughed as Demarcus studied my face.

"How are you really doing though, Mi? You know I can see through that shell you like to keep up."

"I'm actually really confused, Demarcus. I've been thinking about what you've been saying and what we've been doing and…" Before I could complete my sentence, Dionne came rushing through the crowd back to the table, spilling her drink with a look of shock on her face.

"Mayday!" she yelled. "May fucking day!"

"What is wrong with you?" I asked. Dionne motioned her head towards the door.

"What?"

"Bitch, look!" Dionne exclaimed.

I searched through the crowd and that's when I saw him. Jesse stuck out like a sore thumb with his tan double-breasted suit. As he looked around the crowd, I straightened my frame while goosebumps covered my nervous body. Jesse walked through the mingling multitude as Dionne whispered to Demarcus, explaining the situation.

"How's everyone doing?" Jesse asked as he reached our table. "Hello, Dionne."

"What's good," Dionne responded.

"How you doing, brother?" Jesse asked, extending his hand to Demarcus. "I'm Jesse."

"Oh yeah, I've heard about you," Demarcus answered as he shook Jesse's hand. "I'm Cruz."

"Kamila, can we talk?"

"Here, Jesse?" I asked.

"Kamila, please." I sighed as I stood from my seat, following Jesse through the crowd out into the street.

"What are you doing here, Jesse?" I asked.

"What else was I supposed to do? You won't come home. You won't talk to me."

"How did you even know I was here?"

"It wasn't that difficult. I went to Dionne's and you weren't there. I didn't think you'd be at your mother's house so I tried here."

"But I've begged you to come here with me. You were always too busy but you're here now while I'm trying to unwind and take my mind off of everything."

"You used to unwind with me, Kamila."

"And how could I possibly do that with you holding the Bennett Way of Life over my head at every turn?" I asked.

"I don't do that to you."

"Oh, but you do" He gripped my arm as I turned to walk away from him.

"I don't do that to you. Yes, I may ask you to conduct yourself like the girlfriend of a junior partner and yes, I may expect you not to go all Rhonda Rousey on my little sister at a family event but I don't force anything on you and that's not what this is about."

"Please tell me what this is about," I snarled, snatching my arm from him. "Please tell me, Mr. Bennett. Correct me on what I'm saying about my feelings."

"That's not…" Jesse paused to regain his composure as clubgoers began to look on at us while entering and exiting the building. "That's not what I'm saying. I'm saying I didn't come here to talk to you about this Bennett Way of Life you say I'm forcing on you."

"Well, what are we to talk about?" I asked.

"You coming home," Jesse shouted. "You've been running from me since that night with Cassandra. You're with your mom. You're with Silas. You're with Dionne. You're sitting in some club staring into this Cruz guy's face." He paused, studying my reaction to his mention of Demarcus. "Yes, I notice. Your face always gives you away."

"Staring into his face?" I asked, trying my best to ignore what Dionne, Demarcus, my hormones, and apparently now Jesse all seemed to suspect. "He's a childhood friend. Nothing more. And if you recall, I forgave you after Cassandra. I even came home. This is more than that."

"Well come home so we can talk about it," Jesse insisted. I knew he wasn't leaving without me and I definitely couldn't go back to finish my conversation with Demarcus. Not right then.

"Okay," I relented. "I'll meet you at home."

"No," he responded. "You can come with me now. I'll send for your car."

"But what about Dionne? She has to get home."

"Maybe your childhood friend can give her a lift."

Jesse was being super possessive and I wasn't sure I liked it. A small part of me screamed for me to walk away and try to salvage the night with Dionne. I definitely didn't feel comfortable leaving her without a ride home and I knew deep down that Jesse did not want to drive away, leaving me in the same vicinity as Demarcus. It was as if he suddenly knew from looking at us that there was something going on that I was denying to myself. Perhaps there was something going on. Perhaps I gave up on Demarcus far too soon. Maybe Demarcus's infidelity really was a stupid mistake made by an impulsive teenage boy and not the impulsive actions of a grown man I haven't been able to forgive due to deeper issues. At either rate, I wasn't leaving Dionne without ensuring she had a ride home.

As Jesse went back to his car, I walked back inside the club to find Dionne and Demarcus.

"Everything okay?" Demarcus asked.

"Can you give Dionne a ride home?" I asked, dismissing his question. I didn't know if I was okay and telling Demarcus could have been a disastrous idea.

"Why he gotta give me a ride home?" Dionne asked.

"I'll explain later, Dee. Please?" My exhausted, tired eyes begged my sister. I had just got done arguing with Jesse. I didn't want to argue with Dionne and Demarcus. Not now.

"I guess," Dionne relented.

"No problem," Demarcus responded. "But let us know you're okay."

"I'll let Dionne know," I replied. "I probably won't get to you tonight."

Chapter Sixteen

Although he was insistent on me leaving with him immediately so we could talk, the car ride home was deafeningly silent. Jesse barely looked at me and I could hardly look at him. I wasn't sure if I was ready to talk to Jesse or return home. I didn't know what to say to him and I didn't feel comfortable with him being so concerned with Demarcus. During the thirty minute drive home, I passed an occasional glance at him between long stares at the city lights from my window. He stared at the road, giving little expression on his face aside from intermittent flares of his nostrils.

We arrived at our apartment followed by a quiet, uncomfortable walk up the stairs. As we entered our home, I placed my purse on the island bar, preparing to engage in some form of conversation.

"Goodnight," Jesse murmured.

"Goodnight?" I asked. "You insisted I come home immediately so we could talk, you say nothing the entire ride home, and all you have to say to me is goodnight?"

"I really don't know what to say to you, Kamila."

"You knew when you showed up at Exodus."

"I knew *before* I showed up at that club," Jesse snapped. "I hadn't had you as my woman since you left me to go to your mother's. You said you forgave me, you came home, we even made love but I hadn't seen light in your eyes in any of those moments. I had almost forgotten what it was like to see you smile or see that light in your eyes until I walked into that club tonight."

"Jesse..."

"Wait," he interrupted. "Let me finish. I understand, Kamila. Our relationship has hit a bit of a rough patch but when I walked into that club tonight and saw you with that guy, I saw a light in you that I've been missing. I saw the smile that I've been missing. I've been sitting at home calling and begging you to come home and talk to me and I find you smiling at some guy in the club."

"Jesse, you act as if we were on a date or something. Dionne was there."

157

"I know she was there, but I also know what I saw and felt. You're not this arrogant, Kamila. Please don't play dumb with me."

I felt knots forming in my stomach as I looked into his eyes. I could have just let him go to bed and dwell in awkward silence as I was not ready to open this can of worms. By insisting Jesse stay up and talk to me, I metaphorically gave him the can opener.

"Where are you going with this, Jesse?" I asked.

"I think you know."

"I'm not sure I do."

"Who is Cruz?"

A lump formed in my throat. I now had three options. I could continue to play dumb, get defensive, or come clean. Right then, I couldn't do either. All I could do was try to swallow.

"Kamila. Who. Is. Cruz."

"A childhood friend," I replied, attempting to recover from the sheer panic that conquered my body and mind.

"A childhood friend?"

"Yes. He grew up with Dionne and me."

"And that's it?"

"Where are you going with this, Jesse?"

"I just want to know why he got the light and smiles that you used to give me."

"Because I've known him all my life and I'm actually fond of him," I responded. Suddenly, my feelings of guilt and fear were replaced with something different; the realization of my fondness for Demarcus. He was the same man I spent years hating and never wanting to see again but now, I realized that he was the man I wanted to be with.

"I'm just not understanding," Jesse sighed. He paced back and forth, rubbing his hands through his hair. "This isn't sitting right with me, Kamila."

"Why is that, Jesse? You didn't walk into the club to find my head between his legs."

"There it is!" he shouted. "How many more times am I going to have to apologize to you?"

"I'm not asking you to apologize!" I screamed.

"Keep your voice down," he growled.

"Why? You're not!"

"Kamila!"

Our shouts were interrupted by banging on the living room wall. Apparently, the noise we were making disturbed our neighbor, Mr. Lennard.

"You see?" Jesse whispered.

"You know, why don't you just go to bed like you started to?" I snapped. "Is this what you wanted me home for, Jesse? My life has been a wreck and much of that has been because of you. I decide to have a night out with my friends to unwind and for some reason that bothers you. You know what? I don't understand. And I don't think you ever understood me."

"I understand you better than you understand you," he growled, stepping toward me. "I am many things, but I am not a stupid man and you are not telling me everything."

"What if I'm not, Jesse?" I responded. "You wanna know the truth? I'll tell you. Cruz is Demarcus."

"Your ex?"

"My ex." As the words left my mouth, I could feel the hot sting of Jesse's hand slap across my face. I fell back into the wall and grabbed my cheek. *Did this really just happen to me?* I had seen TV shows about this. I had even seen a few of Momma's boyfriends do it to her but I *never* thought that I'd be at the receiving end of physical violence from a man.

"What the fuck type of woman are you?" he growled.

"Did you just hit me?" I cried, pushing myself up from the wall.

"Was my girlfriend in the club smiling in her ex-boyfriend's face?"

"Wait a minute," I responded. "This isn't fair."

"Did you fuck him? Well? Did you?"

I stood against the wall and stared into his face. I could see a rage and a hint of darkness I had never seen in him before. It would have been foolish of me to lie but I was too far away from the bat to risk telling him the truth.

"Answer me!" he growled. My body shook with fear at the sound of his voice. I couldn't make a sound.

"There's my answer. When?"

"I'm not going to talk to you about this now," I whispered. "You hit me. You seriously just hit me."

"Oh fuck your victim bullshit," he snapped. "You hit me! You cheated on me! If you want me to treat you like a woman, act like one. Since you want to act like a slut..."

He rushed up to me and slapped me again. This time it was harder. I screamed in rage and pushed back against him, digging my nails into his face. He grabbed me by my hair and pulled me to the floor. I shouted and kicked at him, trying to pull away from his grip. Mr. Lennard banged against the wall again, but by this point, we were too angry and enthralled in the tussle to care. Mr. Lennard knocked some more as we wrestled around on the floor, hurling insults at each other. After a while, the knocks on the wall were replaced by knocks on the door. Jesse froze with his fist wrapped around the ripped sleeve of my top.

"Yes?" he called, attempting to calm his voice.

"Police. Open up."

Shit!

Jesse glared at me as he released me from his grip and adjusted his clothing. He walked with a strange calmness to the door and opened it as I laid on the ground, cupping my face.

"Yes, Officer?" Jesse asked, opening the door just slightly so the officer couldn't see inside.

"I received a noise complaint," the officer responded.

"Oh, yes," Jesse laughed. "I apologize. I was simply having a discussion with my girlfriend and we got a bit passionate."

"Is your girlfriend here?" the officer asked.

"Yes, sir. She's in the restroom. We've worked out our differences. Everything is fine."

"I think I'd like to confirm that with her," the officer replied.

"Is that really necessary, officer?" Jesse protested. "I apologize for the disturbance but this really is a misunderstanding."

"Sir, are you aware that you have a scratch on your cheek?"

Jesse touched his left cheek where I had scratched him and looked at the bit of blood on his fingertips.

"I hadn't noticed," he responded.

I sat on the floor, listening to the exchange between Jesse and the officer. On one hand, it was ingrained in me not to trust law enforcement but on the other hand, I needed to get out of that apartment and because Jesse insisted I leave my car 30 minutes across town, I had no way out. Logic required me to speak up and get assistance from the police officer so I could get to safety.

"Officer," I called, standing to my feet. I grabbed my purse from the island bar and walked toward the door. Jesse stood in front of me, attempting to block me from the police officer's view.

"Sir, step back," the officer commanded. Jesse stood still.

"Sir," I called from behind Jesse. "I'd just like to leave, please."

"Kamila," Jesse sighed.

"Sir," the officer said. "I'm not going to say it again."

Jesse stepped back and opened the door. I paced in front of him, towards the officer.

"I'd just like to leave, sir," I replied. "I apologize for the disturbance."

The police officer took a look at my battered face and tattered clothing before asking, "Ma'am, did he do this to you?"

I nodded in silence as the tears began to stream from my face.

"Would you like to press charges?" he asked.

"No," I whispered. A small part of me still loved Jesse and wanted to protect him. There were enough brown men caught up in the prison industrial complex and he was one of few brothers who could actually foster change in the criminal justice system when he wasn't just throwing his family name around. Besides, that family name was the very reason why pressing charges would have been completely redundant. His

164

name carried a power that mine didn't. His father probably played golf with whatever judge would get Jesse's case. His father could possibly be poker buddies with the judge who issued my father's prison sentence.

"Are you sure?" the officer asked.

"I'm sure. I just need a ride. My car is across town."

"The farthest I could take you is to the station on Division and Larrabee," he responded. "You can call for a ride there."

"Thank you."

Chapter Seventeen

It felt pretty strange sitting in the back of Officer Jones' squad car. Although I wasn't under arrest, it was against regulation for me to ride in the front seat. I felt a hint of anxiety as I sat behind the cage separating the back seat from the front. As I gazed out the window into the night sky, the events of the night flooded my mind. How did my fairytale love turn into a scene from a Lifetime movie?

"Do you mind if I use my cell phone?" I asked.

"Go ahead," Officer Jones responded. "It's not like you're under arrest."

"Thank you." I pulled the phone from my purse and called the only person I could.

"Hi. I'm sorry to call so late but I'm happy that you're awake."

"I couldn't really sleep," Demarcus responded. "I was worried about you. Are you okay?"

"No, I'm the furthest from okay," I cried. "I need you to do me a huge favor and pick me up at the police station on Division and Larrabee."

"The police station?" he exclaimed.

"Yes."

"What the hell, Mi? Are you in trouble?"

"I'll explain everything when you get here. Please?"

"Of course I'll be there!"

***

Officer Jones allowed me to sit at his desk while I waited for Demarcus. There were papers scattered about along with pictures of a little brown girl with pretty surreal-like eyes. She posed in front of an autumn backdrop, wearing blue and white striped overalls and a white t-shirt. She had dimples as deep as an ocean with her hair in two afro puffs.

"Is this your daughter?" I asked.

"Yes."

"She's beautiful."

"Thank you," he responded. "She starts first grade this coming school year."

"I love that age," I smiled.

I looked around the room as Officer Jones continued typing his report. Although much of the streets were asleep for the night, the police station was lit with activity. Police officers walked in and out, drinking coffee or leading people to their jail cells.

"If you don't mind me asking," Officer Jones asked, "Why didn't you press charges against that guy? It looks like he did a number on you." I hadn't yet looked at my face to see the damage Jesse had done but I figured going to the family building where Silas could see me would have been a bad idea.

"Do you know Gerald Bennett?" I asked.

"Yes, I'm aware of him."

"That was his son. Besides, I've heard how not much is done with domestic violence cases anyway."

"Much of the reason why that happens is that most cases of domestic violence go unreported," Officer Jones responded.

"But his dad is pretty rich and powerful. He'd just get away with it."

"You assume that. As much as it can seem like it's not the case, the law doesn't care who your father is or how much influence you have. Guys like this can sometimes feel entitled to mistreat people because their victims are too intimidated to hold them accountable for their actions."

"Well," I sighed. "This has never happened before. I'm sure it will never happen again."

Officer Jones sighed as his hands fell from his keyboard like weights. He looked down at his lap and shook his head.

"I've been at this job for quite a while, ma'am. I've answered calls of women who refused to press charges and chose to stay. The calls would sometimes come more frequently. It would start with a shouting match and escalate to a slap or a punch and from there, a broken rib. Before you know it, we're calling a coroner. Many women say it will never happen to them but the sad fact is almost half of female homicides are committed by husbands or boyfriends. I'm sure many of them felt it wouldn't happen to them."

His words were sobering. Many thoughts had run through my mind since leaving the apartment I shared with Jesse. He made it seem as if I was making myself out to be a martyr. He felt he was justified in hitting me because I had been with Demarcus. On the other hand, he had been with Cassandra and felt that a mere apology was enough. I was not perfect in this. I probably could have handled things differently, but it was not okay that Jesse hit me, no matter what I had done with Demarcus. I thought about all those women Officer Jones spoke about. I wondered what they did to cause such a reaction from the men who were supposed to love them. I wondered if they did anything at all. What took place in the minds of the men who attacked these women? Why was this sort of violence far more common than I ever realized?

As I continued to mull over my thoughts, I could see a petite female officer guiding Demarcus to Officer Jones and me. His eyes made frantic searches around the crowded room until he spotted me, and I could see tears beginning to form in his eyes as his mouth dropped. He ran to me and I leaped into his arms. He held me in a protective embrace as I sobbed into his chest. Right then, I wasn't concerned with what was appropriate for our relationship. I simply relished in the safety and security that was Demarcus. I had known him since I was a young girl and Denise would have probably sent him back to God if he ever thought of striking a woman. I turned to thank Officer Jones for all of his help and left the station with Demarcus.

***

I sank into the passenger seat of Demarcus's car as he pulled out of the police station.

"He did this to you?" he asked. His voice shook as he fought to hold back tears.

I nodded.

"I'll kill him," he said with a startling sense of calm in his voice.

"You can't do that," I whispered.

"Why the fuck not?" he shouted. "Have you seen your face?"

As I shook my head, Demarcus pulled down the passenger side visor. The mirror lit up and I looked at my left eye, which was a quiet shade of purple and blue. My jaw was swollen and I had a cut in the right corner of my upper lip.

"I wanna see him hit a man like that," Demarcus grumbled.

"It won't help," I protested.

"Oh, it will help. It will help me."

"It will help put you in jail, Demarcus. Denise doesn't need that. I don't need that."

His jaw tightened as he drove southward.

"You can take me to Dionne's," I whispered.

"I'm not about to wake her this time of night,"
Demarcus responded. "You can stay at my place. I'll sleep on
the couch if you want me to, Mi. But right now, I'm going to
need you to stop giving a fuck about what that dude wants
because he clearly could give a fuck about you."

"He figured out that I was with you," I muttered.

"So the fuck what! That gives him license to hit you?
No, fuck that. Did you get to swell his eye when he was
cheating on you?"

"No."

"Then stop making excuses for this cat, Kamila. There
are none."

I stared out of the window thinking over the mess that
had become my life. I still hadn't responded to any of
Momma's calls since finding out about my father and hadn't
heard from Silas at all, but I thought about the conversations I
had with them when I first left Jesse. Momma made many
questionable choices throughout her life and I judged her
every step of the way but there I was. I had become a cheater
and a liar and now the man I envisioned being with for the
rest of my life had assaulted me. I could no longer see the
fairytales and every belief I had about how my life should go
was shattered. I didn't know who I was anymore.

Chapter Eighteen

The sun crept through the blinds of Demarcus's bedroom and woke me from my sleep. I sat up in bed, still a bit sore from my fight with Jesse. When we arrived at Demarcus's house, he had given me some Motrin along with a cup of his mom's Sleepy Time Tea as well as some of his basketball gear to sleep in. I wondered to myself if he had maybe slipped something else into that tea because my body felt as if I had been shot with a tranquilizer gun.

I stood up and tried to keep my steps light on the creaky wooden floor. Stepping toward the window, I peeked through the blinds to see neighborhood children running up and down the street. The clock on Demarcus's dresser read that it was almost noon. Considering the fact that we made it to the house at three in the morning and I had tossed and turned for at least an hour, I realized I didn't sleep as much as I thought.

I turned to see Demarcus standing in the doorway with two Styrofoam plates in his hands.

"I didn't think you'd be up yet," he said. "You should be resting but I wanted to see if you were hungry."

"A little bit," I replied.

"I picked up some breakfast from Denny's."

"Sounds great," I smiled.

I followed Demarcus into the kitchen and we sat at the table. He ordered a Grand Slam breakfast with my eggs just how I liked them, sunny side up. This man still knew my heartbeat after all these years. We sat and ate in silence. The air was heavy as it held the words we wanted to say, and the thoughts and emotions that coursed through our minds and hearts.

"How are you feeling?" Demarcus asked after a few moments of quiet.

"I'm a bit sore but I just feel... I don't know. I feel like he took something from me. He didn't rape me or anything like that, but before that night, I was a different type of woman."

"What do you mean?" Demarcus asked.

"I mean before that night, I didn't realize how dangerous and harmful love can be. I never had a man treat me the way Jesse treated me. The way he looked at me… like I was less than nothing… which I don't understand because he did the same thing he attacked me for doing. Men always have that double standard."

"Not that I'm defending this fuck boy," Demarcus interrupted. "But I gotta speak up for the gender. What's happened between me and you is nothing like what happened with him and old girl. I know you know this."

"Well, I know," I sighed.

"I can only go by what you told me, but it seems like, with old girl, homey was just trying to hit. That's not the same thing that's going on with you and me. At least I'd like to hope it's not."

"It's not." I hadn't wanted to address what was going on between Demarcus and me. I wanted to be loyal to Jesse because I was in a relationship with Jesse but since Demarcus had come back into my life, he was saying and doing all the right things. I couldn't be sure if this was because he had really grown up and really did love me or if he was just doing all of this to get some ass. I didn't know what was what anymore.

"Look," I said. "I know we really haven't had the opportunity to talk about us."

"Not right now," Demarcus interrupted. "Not like this."

We sat in silence again. Demarcus attempted to eat his steak and eggs while his eyes carried the heavy burden of his unspoken thoughts.

"What's on your mind, Demarcus?"

"I just…" he took a heavy sigh and sat back in his chair. "I hated myself for a long time for hurting your heart and this dude bruised your face. Your face, Kamila. I don't think you understand how much you mean to me. And I'm not saying this to run game, but I'm saying this as someone who has known you since we were kids. You and I could just be friends for the rest of our lives but I would never want to see a man treat you like that. You don't deserve it."

"I did cheat on him, Demarcus. With you."

"That doesn't mean you deserved for some dude to go Mayweather on you. Granted, you could say we were wrong for having sex. I'm not sorry and I would never take it back. Dude wasn't here for you. He's not here for you now but you're still defending and being loyal to him. You have love in you that he doesn't deserve."

"He's not a bad person," I muttered.

"Any man that would have your face looking like this is bad enough for me."

We finished eating breakfast and I went back to his room to check my phone. I had about six missed calls from Jesse and two missed calls from Dionne. I called Dionne.

"Are you okay?" she asked as she answered the phone.

"Have I been okay at all recently? I responded.

"Girl, why did Jesse come into the club like that?"

"He wanted me to come home and talk. By the time we made it back to the house, he flipped out because he didn't like the way I was looking at Demarcus. He asked me if I slept with him. I didn't say anything because I didn't want to lie to him. He was already acting weird so I didn't know how he'd react. He pretty much answered the question himself and we got into a fight. The police were called..."

"Wait..." Dionne snapped. "What type of fight?"

"The one you're thinking of."

I could hear a loud gasp over the phone followed by a brief moment of silence.

"Are you okay?"

"My face is a bit bruised but I'm okay," I said.

"I'll kill him. Where are you?"

"At Demarcus's."

"Heffa, why didn't you just come to the house?" Dionne asked.

"Because it was three in the morning."

"Oh, you did good," Dionne laughed. "The only knock on my door I'm getting at three in the morning had better be a knock to give me some ass and you ain't my type."

"Girl, you couldn't afford me," I laughed.

"Whatever, bitch."

"Well, Demarcus is going to take me to pick up my car from over by the club. He had to pick me up from the police station."

"Police station?" Dionne asked.

"Long story."

"Well, when you get your car, come by my place."

"Yes ma'am," I teased.

I ended the call and checked my messages.

"First message sent at 1:43am. 'Kamila. Where are you? You didn't have to leave. I was just upset. It's just… call me.'"

"Second message sent at 2:06am. 'I can't believe you would betray me to the police that way. I had the situation handled, Kamila. You need to call me and let me know you're okay.'"

"Third message sent at 3:22am. 'Okay Kamila. This is getting out of hand. No woman should be out this time of night without anyone knowing of her whereabouts. You need to call me. I hope you're not with this Cruz guy.'"

"Fourth message sent at 6:17am. 'I haven't slept. I'm a wreck. I've had to call off from work. My parents are worried. Mother wants you to give her a call.'"

"Fifth message sent at 7:34am. 'Okay, I get it. You need time. Have your time, Kamila. We will work this out. I promise you.'"

I could feel the knots throb inside my stomach. I could hear the man I fell in love with somewhere mixed within those crazy messages. I still wanted to love him but when I cupped my swollen face, all I felt was rage.

***

When we arrived at Exodus, my car was still parked in the same space I had left it. Demarcus looked on from his car as I walked across the empty parking lot to my car. I looked inside to find a box wrapped in shimmery pink wrapping paper. There was a card attached.

"I behaved foolishly. I can understand if you never want to speak to me again but we have too much history to give up on us now. I love you."

I opened the box to find a Bulgari Serpenti watch that looked like it cost about $10,000.00. I wasn't sure if this meant Jesse was sorry or if he thought I was dumb and cheap enough to be bought. At either rate, I tossed the box towards the back seat and followed Demarcus back toward the neighborhood. Instead of going back to his place, I decided to stop by the family home. As much as I was still not ready to talk to Momma, I hadn't heard from Silas in a while and it was beginning to bother me.

I parked the car in front of the family building and walked up the steps to Silas' apartment. The lights were off and it appeared that no one was home. Momma's apartment was empty too. I pulled out my cell phone to call Silas. No answer. I hoped he wasn't angry with me because I hadn't been by in a while. I pulled my notebook from my purse and wrote a note, letting him know I stopped by and taped it to his TV screen where I knew he would see it.

I got back in the car and decided to go to Dionne's apartment. Switch's *I Call Your Name* played on the radio as I reminisced about visits with Silas to his best friend, Kevin's house. Silas, Kevin, and Kevin's brothers would engage in a trashtalking game of spades while I'd run around the yard with Kevin's children, KJ and Keisha. I hadn't seen much of them since we moved from the projects but recently connected with

Keisha again on Facebook. I knew Silas had kept in touch with Kevin.

I arrived at Dionne's and let myself in. Dionne sat at her desk working on instrumentals. She turned at the sound of the door closing and spun around to look at me.

"What did he do to you?" she cried, jumping from her seat. I stood in place as Dionne examined the scars and bruises on my face. She walked around me as if she were a vehicle owner, examining damage after an accident.

"I'm sure you're done with him," she snapped.

"I guess so," I sighed.

"You have to guess?" Dionne asked. "No, Mila. You are not that girl. We used to talk about those girls."

"We used to do a lot of things we don't do anymore," I responded.

"That's a part of growing Kamila, but this is not growing."

"You're acting like I went back to him," I snapped.

"You act like you're thinking of doing it," she retorted.

"Dee," I sighed. "I never said I was going back to him but I've been with him for a long time. I can't just throw that away."

"If that's the case, what are you doing with Cruz?"

"I don't know!" I rubbed my hands through my hair and plopped down onto the couch. I sat there thinking about my relationship with Jesse while still wearing Demarcus's clothes. The irony was not lost on me.

"Look," Dionne sighed. "You're a smart woman, Kamila. I'm not telling you what to do but I won't pretend I don't think you'd be stupid as hell to go back to that man."

"What am I going to do? I live with him. I have a life with him."

"You act like you can't breathe without that man. Maybe you're a little more dependent on that Bennett money than you'd like to let on."

"What are you saying?" I asked. My blood began to simmer as she said that. Although Jesse did provide me with a life I knew nothing about growing up, I always made an effort to stay true to who I was and not be too dependent on him or his money. I felt as if Dionne was going for a low blow by implying I was dependent on Jesse's money.

"I'm saying he whooped your ass. Look at your face!"

"You know, I didn't come over here for judgment," I shouted. I stood up from the couch and walked back towards the door.

"Look, I'm not trying to judge you," Dionne sighed. "If it sounds that way, I'm sorry. But you watched your mom go through this and if there's even a small piece of you that wants to go back to him, I'm just asking you to seriously not listen to that piece of you. I get it. You've been with him for a long time and you live with him and he supports you but all of his money and dreaminess cannot equate your life, Kamila. Please! I just love and care about you and I don't want to see you hurt."

I released a breath and walked with heavy steps back towards my sister. I collapsed into her arms as she embraced me. Resting my head on her bosom, I could feel the rush of tears spilling from my eyes. Dionne rubbed my back and pet my head as heavy sobs absconded from me.

"Shhh," she said. "It's okay."

"I don't want to fight with you," I whimpered. "I need you. I know I may be having dumb moments right now, but I need you to let me have them. I need you to let me process my thoughts."

"I know," she whispered.

"Everything is so messed up," I cried. "I haven't even had the time to process the truth about my dad, and I haven't talked to Momma or Silas since Momma and I had that nasty fight. Jesse looked at me like I was a whore for sleeping with Demarcus and maybe I am. I don't know."

Dionne pulled my head from her chest and held me at shoulders length so she could look into my eyes.

"No," she said. "You don't get to do that."

"Do what?" I asked.

"You don't get to call my sister a whore. You're human. You fell short and you did something wrong but you do not get to debase yourself or call yourself a whore. Jesse wasn't called a whore or beat to hell for sleeping with that thang, was he?"

"No but…"

"But nothing. My sister is not a whore. You're a woman who got a bit lost and you can get yourself back. But don't do it for Jesse or Cruz or even me. You do it for you. I'm sick of women being put through witch trials for doing the same things these men are celebrated for."

"But Dee, it's different," I said, sinking back into the couch.

"How is it different?"

"I had… have… an emotional connection to Demarcus. Jesse didn't have an emotional connection to

Cassandra. He didn't think of leaving me for Cassandra. He just wanted to hit."

"That makes it okay?" Dionne exclaimed. "Look, I told you when you first slept with Cruz that you needed to figure out what you were doing, but let's not pretend that there wasn't already issues in your relationship that would make you feel the need to seek out someone else."

"We were both wrong," I said.

"You're right. You were. But you didn't violate who he was as a person. What he did to you was criminal. I don't care what you did, he did not have the right to do that to you."

"I guess you're right."

Dionne took a deep breath and walked back towards her desk.

"You're gonna make me need a blunt," she snapped.

"You would have wanted a blunt with or without me," I laughed.

"Maybe but you're working my nerves."

"Shut up, heffa," I laughed. "You love me."

"Bitch somebody has to! Poor child."

I decided to stay the night with Dionne since I already had clothes at her place. Demarcus offered for me to stay with

185

him but I needed time to figure out what I was doing… with him and with Jesse. Dionne and Demarcus were right. Logic dictated I cut Jesse off for good. But it wasn't the watch and it wasn't the fact he supported me financially, it was the time I invested in him. How would I turn that off?

Once Dionne went to bed, I let the mattress out on her sofa bed. I picked up my phone and decided to catch up on Facebook to see what was going on. That was when I saw it.

"Silas Winter was tagged in a status. Keisha Harper: Sending prayers for my godfather, Silas Winter. Praying for a speedy recovery."

What the fuck!

Chapter Nineteen

"It was about time you returned my calls," Momma snapped as I answered the phone.

"What's going on with Silas?" I cried.

"He had a heart attack and he's been in a coma."

"For how long?"

"Four days."

"What the hell?" I shrieked. "You couldn't tell me?"

"I called you," Momma responded. "What more did you want me to do?"

"How about leaving a message? Something! All you said was I acted like I couldn't call you. You didn't say, "Hey Mila, you need to get to the hospital' or 'Hey Mila, Silas is

187

sick.' Why did I have to find out from Keisha on Facebook? She didn't even tell me. She just posted a status."

"If you would have answered when I called, you would have known."

"I can't do this with you," I cried before ending the call.

It was late at night but I needed to see him. I needed to see his face and let him hear my voice so he'd know I was there and loved him. I couldn't lose Silas. I needed for him to pull through and tell me my mess of a life would be okay. I didn't have Big Momma anymore. I had *never* had Momma or either one of my daddies but I always knew Silas would be a staple in my life and that staple was now in danger. I fumed that my mother would be so petty not to leave a message so I would know what was going on. I fumed at myself because I was too wrapped up in my crap and too mad at Momma to go and spend more time with Silas and check on him. All this time, I thought he was upset with me and he was hurting and lying in a hospital bed. I had to see him. I hated that Dionne's lost her driving privileges because I was far too upset to drive. I needed someone and once again, only one person came to mind. Demarcus. I picked up my phone and gave him a call.

"Good to hear from you," he said.

"I'm sorry to call you so late."

"What's wrong?" he asked, hearing the cracking in my voice. "Did homey try to bother you?"

"No," I said. I actually hadn't heard much from Jesse since picking up my car. I sent him a text simply saying I received his gift, but I couldn't be bought. "It's Silas."

"What's going on with Silas?"

"He had a heart attack and has been in a coma for days. Momma didn't even have the decency to tell me."

"I'm sorry to hear that," Demarcus said.

"I guess I'm madder at myself than anything," I sighed. "I've made such a mess of things and I've been so busy dealing with the messes in my life, I didn't take the time to check on him."

"He doesn't blame you."

"I blame me! So many times I've avoided going to see him because I was mad at my momma, or because I knew he'd defend my momma, or because it hurt to be in that building knowing Big Momma wouldn't be there. If I would have just taken a moment and gotten over myself..."

"It wouldn't have stopped him from getting sick, Kamila," Demarcus said. "You can't do that to yourself. He's still here now."

"I'm scared, Demarcus."

"I know. You want me to come over?"

"I need to see him."

"I'll be there in 30."

***

Dionne and I sat on the steps of her apartment building and waited for Demarcus to pull up. I didn't want to leave without telling her what was going on since Silas had a hand in raising her while Jermaine was in prison. Demarcus pulled up and Dionne hopped in back as I sank into the passenger's seat.

"How are you holding up?" he asked, giving me a hug.

"I'm tired, Demarcus," I sighed. "I'm tired of everything."

"I know," he said.

"It's gonna get better, sis," Dionne added, reaching up to rub my shoulder. We drove back across town to the hospital.

"Why didn't she have him transferred to University of Chicago?" I fussed. "Holy Cross is the shittiest hospital on the planet."

"Calm down," Dionne said.

We arrived at the hospital and got on the elevators leading to Silas' room. As we arrived at the cardiac ICU, we could see doctors rushing about. We walked up to the nurse's station.

"Yes," I said. "I'm here to see Silas Winter. I'm his niece."

"Just a moment," the nurse responded. She got up from the desk and walked down the hall where the doctors were gathered. As they walked away, I could see Momma sitting against the wall outside of Silas's room, holding her knees and sobbing. The nurse we had spoken with stopped one of the doctors and said something to him while pointing in my direction. I could feel my heart wanting to run from my chest as the doctor nodded and walked towards me.

"Are you the family of Silas Winter?" he asked.

"Yes," I said, fighting the tears that were beginning to form in my eyes. "I'd like to see my uncle, please."

"I'm sorry, ma'am. Mr. Winter…"

"I'd like to see my uncle, please."

"Kamila," Demarcus said, putting his arm around me.

"No!" I shrieked, pulling away from him. "I'd like to see my uncle, sir. Please."

"Ma'am. I'm afraid Mr. Winter suffered a massive heart attack which caused substantial damage to his heart. Despite our best efforts..."

"No!" I screamed. "This is not happening!" My knees buckled as I felt the urge to vomit. There was no life without Silas. He was my light. That light could not go out. Not now.

Demarcus and Dionne wrapped their arms around me as the doctor went about his business. Momma got up from the floor and walked towards us.

"Mila," she cried. "My brother's gone."

"No!" I shouted. "You do not get to come to me for comfort."

"Kamila," Dionne said.

"No! You get no comfort from me. Fuck you, Sheila!" Momma took a step back as sadness shifted into shock and anger.

"Fuck me?" she growled. "Who the fuck are you talking to?"

"A fucking monster," I snapped.

"Mi," Demarcus whispered. "Don't do this."

"No, Demarcus," I shouted. "*You* don't do this. Everyone has defended her my entire life. She doesn't get to

192

be protected now. What about me? When do I get protected? When does someone stand up for Kamila and say 'No, Sheila, this isn't right'? When? This is what I want to know."

"You are so selfish and disrespectful," Momma snarled.

"I must get it from my momma," I replied. "No. You don't get comfort from me. Big Momma is gone. Silas is gone. They protected you. I won't. I didn't get to be with my uncle during his final days because of you. Why did you ever open your legs if you didn't want to be a mother?" She pulled her hand back and slapped me with all her might. I fell backward and my hands formed into fists as I caught my balance. Dionne leaped in front of me.

"No, Kamila," she said. "She's still your mother."

"Opening your legs and pushing doesn't make you a mother," I snapped. I looked at my mother as Demarcus stood in front of her, holding her back from me.

"As far as I'm concerned, the last of my family just died today. You don't exist to me. Don't call me. Don't speak to me. Period." I turned around and stormed back towards the elevators as Dionne and Demarcus ran behind me.

The three of us were silent as we walked back to the car. I stared out the window into the night sky as the rest of the world melted away from me. There was a time when I was innocent and believed in magic. My sense of everything good in life was slowly slipping away before my eyes and there was nothing I could do to stop it. I could no longer go to Silas for advice. I couldn't go to him and ask him what to do about Jesse or Momma or Jermaine. My father figure and voice of reason was no longer living.

"My momma is in assisted living," Demarcus said, breaking the silence. "I'd give anything to take the cancer from her. If I could trade places with her and be in that bed instead of her, I'd do it in a moment. Your momma is alive and well and this is what you do."

"Don't do that, Demarcus," I responded. "Denise is nothing like my mother."

"Isn't she? Did your mother give you life?"

I continued to stare out the window without response.

"Well, did she? That's what she has in common with my mother. She carried you. She felt you kick. She felt the pain of bringing you into this world, Kamila. That's what my mother and your mother have in common. As much as I love my mother, she wasn't perfect. There were times she drove me crazy but I would never do to her what you just did to your mother, Mila. I'm feeling your anger and I'm feeling your pain, but it's fucked up what you did."

"I hate to do this, but I gotta agree with Cruz," Dionne added.

"Oh, now y'all wanna team up on me?" I snapped. "Stop the car."

"Kamila," Demarcus sighed. "It's the middle of the night in the hood. Stop being crazy."

"No," I said. "I meant what I said at that hospital. Everybody defends her. Nobody thinks about me. If y'all want to jump on the bandwagon, then fuck y'all too."

"Kamila, you're angry and I get it," Dionne said.

"No, you don't get it. You still have the woman who raised you. Your dad may be in prison but he's still here. Sheila has never been there for me. Never! I need y'all to be on my side and if you won't do it, fuck y'all. Just take me back to my car."

We rode the rest of the way in complete silence. When we arrived at Dionne's, I got out of the car without saying a word to either of them and jumped directly into my own car.

"Where are you going, Kamila?" Dionne asked.

I drove away without an answer.

Chapter Twenty - Demarcus

After ensuring Dionne was safely inside her apartment, Demarcus made the long, lonely drive back home. He often enjoyed late night traffic as there weren't many cars on the road and the streetlights were timed. He wondered if he was a bit too hard on Kamila. After all, she was grieving. Silas played a major role in her life, and whenever the time came for his mother to pass on, he couldn't be sure he wouldn't overreact. However, after everything his mother had been going through, he couldn't bear to watch while Kamila take having a healthy mother for granted, no matter what type of mother Sheila may have been. But still, it was pretty late at night. He didn't know where she was or if she was safe. She was pretty upset with him, Dionne, and her mother and those are the usual people she would turn to unless... No. She wouldn't go back there. She couldn't. Panic flooded Demarcus's body as he pulled his car to the side of the road just blocks away from his home. He pulled out his phone and called Kamila.

"Shit!" he exclaimed to himself. "No answer." He ended the call and tried to call back two more times. Still nothing. She didn't want to talk to him and part of him understood, but she needed someone who cared about her and could keep her safe. The place he suspected she was headed was anything but safe.

As much as he wanted to go look for her, Demarcus pulled his car back onto the road and continued home. If she didn't want to talk to him, he was sure she didn't want to see him. He thought back to the high school days when Kamila would get upset and not speak to him for weeks. She could be pretty brutal. But silent treatment or not, there was a possibility she was allowing her grief to put her in danger and that did not sit well with him.

As he walked up the steps to his home, he pulled his phone from his pocket and called Dionne.

"What's up, Cruz?" she asked.

"I'm sorry it's so late but…"

"You're worried about Mila," Dionne responded.

"Yeah. You don't think…"

"I do."

"What should we do?" Demarcus asked, standing in the doorway.

"I'm not sure," she replied. "She's not answering her phone. I don't know what she's gonna do with this state of mind but I hope she didn't go back to him."

"Should we go over there?"

"What would it do, Demarcus? She's a grown woman. We can't pick her up and throw her ass over our shoulders. Well, you could, but I ain't doing the shit."

"I don't feel right going to sleep not knowing if she's okay."

"I don't either. So I guess we can stay up and worry together."

"I'm on my way back," he said.

Demarcus walked back out of the doorway and locked the door behind him. The cool night breeze caressed his face as he walked back to his car and headed to Dionne's. His temples began to throb as his mind flashed back to Kamila's face in that police station. He thought of what that fuck boy had done to her beautiful face. The possibility of her being in Jesse's arms made Demarcus feel a mixture of fear and anger. He was angry because he wanted to bash Jesse's face in. He was angry because Kamila would do something so rash and foolish in her grief. He was angry that his big mouth and feelings about his mom clouded his ability to help Kamila deal with her grief. He drove with his mind flooded with thoughts as if in a trance. In what seemed to him like no time, he was parked in front of Dionne's apartment building. He sat for a few moments in a daze, rubbing his temples. A knock on the passenger side window interrupted his reverie.

"You planning on getting out of the car, fool?" Dionne asked.

"Yeah, yeah," Demarcus stuttered as he got out of the car. "Have you been able to talk to her?"

"Nothing," she responded. The two of them climbed over the sleeping bum on the steps and walked up to her apartment.

"You don't worry about coming out here at night with these fools around here?" Demarcus asked.

"Boy, I'm not worried about these fools. You know how the hood works. They don't mess with the ones they know."

"That's what you think," Demarcus responded, watching his surroundings. Demarcus never felt comfortable on the west side. Although he hadn't been involved with the streets since moving back to the city, he was aware that walking onto the wrong block at the wrong time could very well cost him his life. He was used to the south side. He knew the law of the land around there. He didn't feel he belonged on the west side.

Demarcus and Dionne walked into the apartment. Demarcus took a seat on the couch while Dionne went into the kitchen to fix a pot of coffee.

"If we're pulling an all-nighter, we're gonna need some coffee," she replied. "Wait… on second thought, that didn't sound right."

"It's all good," Demarcus laughed. "I know that's not what you meant. Now that I think of it, I don't think I've ever heard you talk to anybody using innuendo but if you did, it wouldn't be me."

"I don't kiss and tell, Cruz," Dionne answered. "You take cream and sugar?"

"Yeah, both," Demarcus responded. Dionne added the cream and sugar to Demarcus's coffee while leaving her coffee black. She walked into the living room with the two steaming hot cups, giving one to Demarcus and then walked over to the opposite couch, sipping from her cup.

"You surely don't. I guess I can respect that though," Demarcus said, taking a sip of coffee. "Kissing and telling have caused a lot of trouble in people's lives."

Dionne took another sip of coffee and placed the cup on the table.

"You really care about her, don't you?" she asked.

"I never stopped," he responded.

"So why'd you do it?"

Demarcus released a hard sigh, rubbing his free hand across his head.

"I was young and dumb," he said. "My boys were making fun of me, calling me sprung. They knew how Ms. Mary kept Kamila in church and there was no way I was getting any from her. I tried but she wasn't going. Then there was Janette. The girl was just putting it on a plate for me. I knew it was wrong the minute I did it. It felt like that day just ruined everything."

"She was hurt for a long time after that."

"I know," Demarcus said, lowering his eyes. A wave of sadness took over him as he remembered the day Kamila confronted him. "The truth is, I hurt myself. In a way, I've always done that. I didn't feel like I deserved her in my life. Hell, Sheila knew it."

"Boy, Sheila hated anyone who was with Kamila," Dionne laughed.

"But it seemed like all of y'all turned on me."

201

"I didn't turn on you, Cruz… Okay, well maybe I kinda did, but she was my girl. Chicks before dicks and all… but for what it's worth, I didn't think you were a bad guy."

"But what if I was?"

"Why would you say some foolishness like that?" Dionne asked.

"I mean… if I never would have hurt Kamila, if I never would have lashed out at Moms and got into the trouble I got into, maybe Moms would have never got sick and maybe Kamila wouldn't have ever been with Buster Brown over there."

"And maybe pigs would fly and the cow would jump over the moon," Dionne retorted. "You don't know what could have happened."

"Yeah, I know," Demarcus said. "I just can't help but feel like this is my fault."

"You didn't kill Silas. Kamila is grieving and she's lashing out. You were right to check her on the shit she said to Sheila. If you wouldn't have said it, I still would have said it. She was wrong, point blank period."

"Maybe."

"Cruz," Dionne said, leaning over towards him. "She was wrong."

Demarcus felt the tears wanting to form but quickly blinked them away. After all, he was a man. He didn't think it would be a good look for him to cry in front of Dionne.

"Anyway," he said, attempting to change the subject. "Have you been able to talk to her?"

"What do you think?" Dionne smirked, pursing her lips.

"I had to ask," he sighed, pulling his phone out to call again. The phone rang and rang until the voicemail picked up.

"Kamila," he said. "Please call me or at least call Dionne. We're worried about you. We haven't slept. Please just let us know you're okay."

Sunlight began to beam through the blinds as Demarcus began to nod in and out of sleep. He blinked for what he thought was about a minute and opened his eyes two hours later. He looked around and grabbed his phone from the coffee table, hoping to have received some sort of word from Kamila. Nothing. He laid back and rubbed a hand over his tired face as he heard Dionne's voice coming from the hallway.

"I know, baby," she whispered. "It's just so much going on with Kamila and Demarcus is over… I miss you too… I'll meet up with you as soon as we make sure my sister's okay… I love you too… Bye."

Demarcus quickly closed his eyes, pretending he was still asleep. He wondered why Dionne was so secretive about her love life. Could she have had some form of embarrassing fetish? Was the dude ugly? Did she find herself a prison pen pal? He didn't know, but whatever it was, he wasn't going to try to find out. At least not right then.

He opened his eyes again, letting out a loud fake yawn so Dionne would know he was awake. Picking up his phone, he tried to call Kamila again.

"Hello?" a male voice answered.

"I'm looking for Kamila," Demarcus said as anxiety pulsated through his body.

"Ooh… you must be the ex," Jesse laughed. "Hey, ex. I'm the current."

"Where's Kamila?" Demarcus asked, standing from the couch. Dionne walked back down the hall into the living room, staring at Demarcus in shock.

"Oh, my baby's in bed," Jesse laughed. "I made sure she got some rest. The two of us had such a long workout."

"Motherfucker," Demarcus growled. "If you touch her…"

"Why?" Jesse interrupted. "She's mine. I can touch any part of her I want. What, you thought because you played

Captain Save-A-Hoe for a night, you could take her away from me? Imagine that!"

"Did you just call her a hoe?" Demarcus asked. Flashes of red blinked before his eyes as pure rage overtook him.

"Hoe?" Dionne snapped. "I got your hoe, Mr. Gumbel."

"You know its lights out when I see you, right?" Demarcus said.

"I highly doubt that," Jesse responded. "Just face the facts, Mr. Cruz. The better man won."

"The better man?" Demarcus laughed. "Bitch, you gotta be fucking kidding me."

"You're hearing my voice on her phone, aren't you?" Jesse asked. "That should tell you something, bro. She's in bed right now. I'll be sure to tell her you called though. Or maybe I won't."

Suddenly, Demarcus could hear Kamila's voice in the background - and then what sounded like arguing. He could hear Jesse giving Kamila the phone and yelling at her, telling her what to say. He could hear her frightened breaths pulsating through the phone. He could feel her fear.

"Kamila, are you okay?" he asked. "What are you doing there?"

"I…"

His blood boiled as he heard Jesse yelling again in the background.

"I'm coming to get you," Demarcus said. "You don't have to say anything. If you want to tell me you're back with him, tell me, but I'm on my way."

"Okay," Kamila whispered. "We're back together."

"I'm on my way," Demarcus said.

His arms shook as he ended the call. He didn't care about protecting his masculinity. He was angry. He was afraid. The woman he loved was in the same danger she was in the night he picked her up from the police station. He pictured her face that night. He pictured his mother's face the many nights his father beat her. He rubbed his side, thinking of the kicks he would take to the ribs as a boy. He didn't know Jesse well, but he knew enough to hate him with every fiber of his being. Hot tears stung his cheeks as he clutched his phone, calling his cousin Nadia.

"What's going on?" Dionne asked. Demarcus held up a finger to Dionne as Nadia answered his call.

"Hello?" Nadia said.

"I need you and Will to get dressed because I'm coming to get you."

"What's up?" Nadia asked. "His brother's over."

"That's good," Demarcus responded. "The more, the merrier."

"Demarcus, what's going on?" Nadia asked.

"This motherfucker called Kamila a hoe and threatened her while I was on the phone listening to the entire thing. I'm going to get her."

"He threatened her?" Dionne shouted.

"I need y'all with me," Demarcus continued. "Partially because I don't know what I'm walking into and partially because I'm gonna need y'all to keep me from killing this piece of shit."

"We'll be ready," Nadia replied. "Just calm down. Kamila will be okay."

"Just be ready when I blow," he said.

"Fuck that," Dionne snapped. "I'm coming, too. And I got something in case he wants to get stupid." Dionne rushed down the hall to her bedroom as Demarcus ended his call with Nadia. He huffed and puffed, swinging his fists into the air as he tried not to punch a hole through Dionne's wall.

He couldn't help but feel it was his fault. If he was too late to get to Kamila, he wasn't sure if he could forgive himself.

Dionne ran back into the living room wielding a pocket knife.

"You breathe, baby," she said, breezing past Demarcus to grab a head wrap for her hair. "We got this, even if that motherfucker ends up in a bag." Demarcus knew that Dionne was joking about actually murdering Jesse but part of him didn't mind sending Jesse's soul to God.

Chapter Twenty-One

I sat in my car, staring at the steering wheel. In an act of anger mixed with a bit of stupidity, I found myself parked in front of the apartment I shared with Jesse. I had not seen him since our fight, but after lashing out at my mother, my sister, and Demarcus, I didn't know where else to go. My mind wandered back and forth, wondering if I should go up the stairs to reconcile with Jesse or if I should find some common sense and drive away. Hours went by as I sat in the car, debating on what to do. Dionne and Demarcus took turns blowing up my cell phone but in my state of grief, I didn't want to talk to either of them.

The sun rose as the street began to awaken. Jesse walked out of the building wearing a white muscle tee and gray sweatpants, preparing for his morning run. He put his earbuds in his ears and started to run but stopped once he noticed my car. He walked over and tapped the driver side window. I rolled the window down.

"How long have you been here?" he asked.

"A couple of hours," I replied.

"Why are you just sitting in the car?"

"Because I don't know if I should be here."

"Of course you should be," he said. "This is your home."

"Is it? I don't know. There was a time I thought it was."

"It can be your home if you want it, Kamila."

"I don't know if I want it," I said. "I don't know if I belong anywhere anymore."

Jesse opened the door and wrapped his arms around me as he kissed my temples.

"You belong with me," he said. "I'm sorry for what our relationship has come to. I'm sorry for my actions. I should have never hit you. You're a treasure to me." I melted at his words. Every voice in my head screamed, wanting me to push him away and drive for my life but my emotions and hormones screamed for him. I wanted all the pain to go away and Jesse was the man I was supposed to be with. I wouldn't be cheating with him and I didn't want to worry about defining things. I just wanted all the hurt that had become my life to go away. I turned my face to him and kissed him as he rubbed a gentle hand across my bruised eye.

"I don't know if I can trust you," I whispered. "But I don't want to be alone right now. Silas… he's… I can't even say the words." Uncontrollable trembles overtook my body as Jesse held me close.

"You don't have to say anything right now," he said. "Just come home. We'll take it from there." I nodded as I took the keys from the ignition. Jesse wrapped his arm around my waist and guided me up the steps to our apartment. I looked around at the place I hadn't been to since our fight. I looked at the wall I fell against after he hit me and the couch on which he sat while cheating on me with Cassandra. When I made the drive, I thought coming home would give me some sort of comfort after fighting with everyone in my life. Now that I was there, all I wanted to do was vomit. I pulled away from Jesse and ran towards the bathroom to throw all of my anxiety into the toilet. Jesse rushed behind me and looked on from the bathroom door.

"Are you okay?" he asked.

"Okay and I don't belong in the same sentence," I responded, looking up from the toilet. I could barely look at him. It was then I knew I couldn't be with Jesse anymore.

Every time I looked into his eyes, I relived the memories of our last horrible night together. Going back to him was a major mistake.

"You've had a rough night," Jesse said. "Why don't you get into bed and get some rest?"

"I am pretty tired," I said. I brushed my teeth and rinsed the taste of vomit from my mouth. I took a shower and let the hot water rinse the tension from my body. When I was done, I slipped into my pale blue nightie and got into bed. It didn't take much for me to fall asleep.

Sometime later, I was awakened by Jesse's voice. I assumed he had decided to work from home so he could stay with me. I shifted under the covers while staring at the ceiling until the words he said into the phone began to register in my mind.

"You're hearing my voice on her phone, aren't you? That should tell you something, bro. She's in bed right now. I'll be sure to tell her you called though. Or maybe I won't." *Crap!* He was talking to Demarcus on my phone. I jumped up from the bed and ran into the living room.

"Oh hey baby," Jesse flashed a sinister smile. "You awake? Hey Demarcus. She's awake. She'll tell you now that she doesn't want to talk to you." Jesse held my phone out to me.

"What are you doing?" I asked.

"Go on, Kamila," he said. "Tell your ex that you don't want to talk to him anymore. Tell him that we're back together."

"Why are you answering my phone?" I asked.

"Why does that matter? Tell him."

"I don't know that we're back together, Jesse."

"Oh, right. Are you really going to leave me for this fool? Stop playing, Kamila. Tell him. Now." I recognized the look on Jesse's face and immediately felt anxious. I inched toward him and took the phone.

"Kamila, are you okay?" Demarcus asked. "What are you doing there?"

"I..."

"Tell him, Kamila. Tell him we're back together."

"I'm coming to get you," Demarcus said. "You don't have to say anything. If you want to tell me you're back with him, tell me. But I'm on my way."

"Okay," I muttered. "We're back together."

"I'm on my way," Demarcus said.

"Okay," I replied. "I'm sorry." I ended the call. Jesse walked over to me and hugged me, kissing my forehead.

"That's my girl," he said. "You belong with me. No other man is gonna do for you what I do." I was hoping that was a promise.

An hour later, Jesse took my car to pick up some Chinese food he had ordered for lunch. I assumed he took my car because he was afraid I'd try to leave while he was gone. I sat on the couch, staring at the blank television screen when I heard a knock at the door. I rushed over to answer. Demarcus, Will, Dionne, Nadia, and Will's twin brother Philip stood at the door.

"Where is he?" Demarcus snarled.

"He went to get lunch," I said. "He took my car."

"Get your stuff," he commanded. I rushed to the bedroom and started to grab my things. I could feel the panic rushing through my veins as I moved as fast as I could, hoping we'd all be gone from the apartment before...

"What the hell?" I could hear Jesse's voice from where I stood. "What are you people doing in my apartment? I can call the police on all of you."

"Please call them, motherfucker," Dionne snapped. "I want them to be here and bring a body bag for what you did to my sister."

"Kamila!" Jesse shouted. "Kamila, get in here now!"

I stood frozen in the doorway of the bedroom and looked on as Jesse stood with a puffed-out chest in front of Demarcus, who stood at least four inches taller than him.

"You know you talk really tough for someone who's outsized and outnumbered," Demarcus smirked. Jesse looked back at me.

"Did you invite this trash into my house?" he snarled as if foam would come from his mouth.

"I got your trash," Dionne said.

"Fall back, Dee," Demarcus smiled. "I got him. Call the police, homeboy. We're here to help our friend leave a violent situation. The proof is on her face. And I'm pretty sure the law is already familiar with you from the last time Mila was here."

"Kamila told you she didn't want you anymore. We're back together." Jesse's voice faltered like a scared little boy who faced losing his favorite toy. I looked into the creases on his face and I no longer saw the Bennett Family Way of Life or even the monster that dragged me around the living room

215

floor. I was looking into the face of a scared, insecure little boy.

"I said that for you, Jesse," I said. I walked into the living room where my sister, my friend, and his friends and family were standing. They were brave enough to come out to stand up for me. The least I could do was stand with them.

"I said that for you. I didn't want you to snap and hit me again."

"Kamila," Jesse whimpered. "I love you."

"You don't love me," I said. "You possess me. You buy me things as a means to keep me. That type of stuff may work for someone like Cassandra but it doesn't work for me. I immediately regretted coming here the second I walked into this room and looked at that wall."

"I wouldn't have done it if you weren't being a whore," he snapped. His eyes became possessed with an anger I was beginning to know well. "Let's be honest. You're no damsel in distress. You got what you had coming to you for cheating on me and being a fucking slut. If you want to go, you can leave. I won't stop you. But don't you ever come…" Before Jesse could finish talking, Demarcus leaped forward and punched him in the mouth. Jesse fell backward onto the island bar as Dionne jumped up and down, squealing and clapping her hands.

"Hell yeah!" Dionne exclaimed. "I'm glad somebody shut his ass up. I wanted to do it but I just got my nails done."

"My dude, what you're not going to do is keep calling her out of her name," Demarcus said. Jesse pulled himself up from the bar and put his hand over his mouth.

"Do you know who I am?" Jesse cried. "I can have you thrown under the jail for this!"

"Do it and you'll be in the cell next to him," I snapped, stepping towards Jesse. "I still have Officer Jones' contact information. We got to know each other very well on the ride to the police station. He'd be happy to come lock your punk ass up."

"Just get out of my place," Jesse grumbled.

Will, Nadia, Philip and Dionne helped me grab my things while Demarcus kept guard to make sure Jesse didn't try anything on the way out. We loaded some things into Demarcus's car and the rest into mine.

"Yo Will," Demarcus said. "Can you drive my car? I'm gonna ride with Mila."

"Okay, cool," Will said.

"Well hell," Dionne said. "I'll ride with y'all." Demarcus gave Dionne a look indicating he wanted to be alone with me.

"Or I can ride with Will and them," she said. "Y'all don't mind if I smoke, do you?"

"Hell no," Philip exclaimed. "As long as you're sharing." They all got into Demarcus's car and pulled off. Demarcus took my keys and got behind the driver's seat of my car.

"You sit in the passenger's seat and rest," he said. I did as instructed as he started to drive. "What were you thinking about, Kamila? Why did you come back here?"

"I wasn't thinking," I said. "I was so hurt about losing Silas and I was mad at everyone. I hated Momma, I hated me, and I hated you and Dionne for defending Momma. I wasn't thinking straight when I came back here. At first, I felt it was something I should have done but the moment I walked into that living room, all those memories came flooding back and I knew I had made a mistake."

"Kamila, do you know how hard it was for me to pick you up from a police station and see your face the way it was?"

"I could imagine," I responded.

"I don't think you can," he said. "If you could, you wouldn't have come back here and put Dionne and me through this."

"I didn't mean to bring you two into this," I muttered.

"Girl, shut up," he laughed. "We didn't mind coming to get you. I mean we were scared to death worrying about where you were and if you were okay. And when I called your phone and he answered, my heart fell into my stomach. You may not feel like you have family left but you have Dionne and me, no matter what happens with us."

"I guess you're right," I said. "And I guess you and Dionne were right about my mom. I just didn't want to hear it. I didn't mean it when I cursed y'all out."

"We know," Demarcus replied. "We knew you were just hurting. We knew you didn't mean what you said to your mom either."

"I felt like I meant it."

"You didn't," Demarcus said. "I know you and your mom have your issues and what not but you didn't mean what you said to her at that hospital. If something happened to your mother, you'd never forgive yourself. You can't leave things how they are, Kamila."

"You're right again," I sighed. "Don't get used to hearing that all the time."

"I won't," he smiled.

"Speaking of leaving things how they are, I feel like we need to talk."

"Oh yeah?"

"Yes," I responded. "We haven't had the chance to talk about me and you."

"I guess it's just never been the right time," Demarcus shrugged. "Look, Kamila. You know how I feel about you. I never stopped loving you. You know I want you back in my life, but I want you to do it because you're in a good frame of mind and you want me too. I don't want you to do it on a rebound or feel that you owe me something. Everything I've done for you, I'd do if we were only friends."

"I don't feel obligated to be with you, Demarcus."

"Good. You shouldn't."

"I don't."

"Fine."

"Fine then," I said. We drove in silence the rest of the way to Demarcus's house where everyone else was waiting. Demarcus parked the car and moved his hand toward the door to exit. I leaned toward him, giving him a passionate kiss. He wrapped his arms around me and returned my kisses. I stopped for a moment and touched my forehead to his, looking into his eyes.

"It's not that I feel obligated to be with you," I whispered. "It's that it took years of us being apart and years of being with the wrong man for me to learn where I'm meant to be. You broke my heart before. Please don't do it again."

"I can't promise I won't," he said, cupping my face. "I can promise that I'll do everything in my power to protect your heart." We kissed again until we were interrupted by a knock on the window.

"Um, Romeo and Juliet, can you get the fuck out the car, please?" Dionne smirked. I flipped her the bird as Demarcus and I got out of the car and joined everyone else as they waited at the front steps. Dionne stepped behind Demarcus and me and grabbed my hand, pulling me backward.

"I knew y'all would get together," she laughed.

"Heffa no you didn't," I snapped. "You were hating from the beginning."

"No, I wasn't. I was just telling you to make sure you were done with Carlton Banks before you got too serious with Cruz."

"Well, it's all good now," I sighed. "At least something is all good now."

Chapter Twenty-Two

After the craziness at the apartment where I used to live with my now ex-boyfriend, Jesse, we joined everyone else at my current boyfriend's place for a game of dominoes and a vast amount of drinking.

"I'm glad y'all got together," Nadia smiled. "He really loves you."

"I don't think I ever stopped loving him," I replied. It was nice to be with someone whose family was warm, accepting and loving. It was a welcomed change from the cold sterile Bennett family. I was sure Jesse's family was consoling him while telling him he was better off without me and maybe that was true. I knew for sure I was much better off without him.

The sun began to set over the humid night. Will and Demarcus were immersed in a game of Mortal Kombat while the rest of us were engaged in a game of spades. I got up from the table to get a glass of water and Philip rushed into the kitchen behind me.

"Excuse me, Kamila," he said. "I wanted to ask about your sister."

"What about her?" I asked.

"Do you know if she's seeing anyone?"

"To be honest, I don't have a clue. For someone who's always very much in my business, Dionne's kind of secretive about her dating life."

"Do you think I should try and talk to her?"

"That's up to you," I replied. "I'll warn you though. She's a live wire. If she curses you out, try not to take it to heart."

"Thanks," he said.

The two of us walked back into the dining room and returned to our spades game. Nadia looked at me and smiled as she dealt a new hand.

"I got my cousin-in-law this time," she said. "We're about to spank y'all asses!" I blushed at her words. Cousin-in-law. Demarcus and I had just got back together and this

223

woman was already welcoming me to the family. It felt flattering.

"Y'all not ready for this," Dionne laughed. "Philly and I got this game on lock! Ain't that right, Philly?"

"That's right, baby," Philip smiled as he picked up his cards.

"How much do you bid then, Philly?" I laughed. He studied his hand and looked to Dionne for validation.

"I got 5," he said.

"I got 4," Dionne added.

"Okay, we're gonna see," I smirked. We got into our game. I was confident because as much trash as Dionne talked, she was horrible at spades. She couldn't go one single game without reneging and as I suspected, Nadia and I spanked their asses.

"We got you next game," Dionne snapped.

"You're a sore loser," I laughed. "Plus it's getting late. I should probably get going soon." Demarcus heard me from the living room and paused his game.

"Going?" he asked. "You know you're welcome to stay."

"I appreciate that, Demarcus. But we just got back together. I don't want us to immediately jump into living together. Besides, you were right. I need to go make things right with my mom." Demarcus walked over to me and wrapped his arms around me.

"She's beautiful and sensible," he smiled as he kissed my forehead. "I don't want you to leave, but that's a very good reason to go ."

"I guess I'll go with you," Dionne added, getting up from the table.

"Wait!" Philip called, standing to join Dionne. "I was wondering maybe if you were free some time, we could get together?"

"Wait," Dionne laughed. "Let me stop you, Philly. You're cool and all and we can hang out but you've got the wrong equipment for me."

"Wait, what?" I exclaimed.

"You've never seen me with a man, sis," Dionne said. "There's a reason for that."

"You said it was because you didn't kiss and tell," I snapped.

"Yes, because black folks are stupid as hell and everybody don't need to know my business. But yes, I'm a lesbian." The room grew quiet as we took in this new information.

"Bitch," I snapped. "Why didn't you ever tell me?"

"Because I didn't know how you'd react," she responded.

"Seriously? You're still my sister."

"That doesn't mean anything. My girlfriend's sister completely disowned her when she came out. Her mother too. Plus I suspect my own mother may be planning some sort of exorcism for me with her bible study group."

"That has nothing to do with me," I replied. "I love you no matter what. And wait… girlfriend? Who told your little fast ass you could have a girlfriend?"

"Um, I'm grown, bitch."

"No, fuck that!" I laughed. "It's my turn to get all up in your business. I need to examine this bitch to make sure she's right for my sister."

"I didn't mean any disrespect," Philip interrupted.

"No problem," Dionne said. "You didn't know."

"Can I watch?" Demarcus asked.

"Hell no!" I snapped. "Nasty ass!"

"And yet you're with me," he laughed.

"And I'm really about to go question my life choices."

Dionne and I left my car and clothes parked at Demarcus's and walked to the family home. The living room smelled like a distillery as Momma sat on the couch, nursing a bottle of gin while watching a video of the last family reunion we had before Big Momma passed away. She looked up at Dionne and me.

"I thought I was dead to you," she said. I looked down at the frail woman who gave me life as she sat on the couch, washing her sorrows away with gin. I walked around to the opposite side of the couch and sat beside her as Dionne welcomed herself to some of the bereavement meals that were brought over by well-wishers.

"I didn't mean any of that stuff I said, Momma," I said. "I was hurt and angry. It doesn't mean I should have said what I said, but that's what it was. Momma, we got issues. We have a steamer trunk of issues but we gotta stop all this back and forth that we do. Big Momma and Silas are gone. We're all we've got. We need each other."

"I agree."

"Momma, I need you to try and cut back on this drinking that you do. You can't keep running from the pain. Neither of us can keep running. It will only keep chasing us."

227

"There was a time when I would have never touched a drop of this stuff," Momma said. "Momma had a younger brother who died in his thirties long before you were born. He died from cirrhosis of the liver. He was an alcoholic. I used to swear I never wanted to be like him. It wasn't until Royal died when I even thought about touching a bottle. You've spent your entire childhood resenting me, Kamila. But you never actually took the time to see things from my perspective."

"How could I when I didn't know?"

"I didn't want you to know," she responded. "I didn't want you to carry this burden. I didn't want you to know this pain. I may have made my mistakes and you may think I'm a lousy mother but I didn't want you to know the darkness that surrounded the time you were born. That was one of the darkest, scariest times of my life. I had to face my mother and tell her that her child was about to have a child all while staying silent about the fact that I had been with an older, married man and my actions caused the death of a young boy who was the love of my life. I loved Royal and he's dead because of things I've done. I couldn't bring myself to tell an adult all of that, let alone my child."

"So this is why you started drinking?"

"It's been hard to live with. I've done the best I could do with the time I've had, Kamila. I haven't always done right by you, but I've done the best I could do."

"I think I understand, Momma," I replied. "I've lived my life trying to be the antithesis of you. When I went off on you, I was mad at myself. I wasn't around for Silas' last days because I was avoiding you. I hated myself for that. It was hard for me to accept the truth of everything that happened and it was harder for me to accept our last conversation before Silas got sick. I just hate that my last moments with Silas were spent with him being the referee between you and me."

"Child, hush," she said. "That man knew you loved him and he loved you."

"I thought he was mad at me when he wasn't answering my calls."

"He wasn't mad at you. He was mad at me. And I can't really say I blamed him. He didn't know I was with Jermaine and he was upset about me not talking to you before you went out to that prison. You're best friends with his daughter. I really should have known you'd find out sooner or later."

"Yeah," I responded. "I still don't know how I feel about that. I've spent my life loving and mourning for Royal."

"You still can," she said. "But you owe it to yourself to get to know Jermaine. He can tell you things about yourself I can't."

"Maybe so," I replied. "What's going on with the funeral arrangements?"

"I don't know," Momma said. "Silas didn't have life insurance and we don't have any money. I want him buried next to Momma but we may not be able to afford it."

"We may be able to," I replied. "Just let me try to work some things out. But for now, I'm gonna go get some sleep. I'm going to need to stay down at Big Momma's for a while."

"Welcome home," Momma said.

Chapter Twenty-Three - Dionne

Dionne's stomach fluttered with excitement. She hadn't planned on blurting out her secret in a room full of strangers. Adriana and she had talked at length about it being time for Kamila to know the truth and she agreed it was long overdue but with everything Kamila had going on in her life, it was never the right time. When they were all at Cruz's place just hanging out, it was the most relaxed and happy she had seen Kamila. Kamila was able to relax, which helped Dionne relax and things just happened from there. She was relieved Kamila didn't have the same reaction as her mother or Adriana's family. She was happy she could finally be herself around Kamila. She and Adriana no longer needed to sneak around her own apartment.

When she arrived home, Adriana was seated on the couch, sipping a cup of chamomile tea. Adriana's amber eyes glittered like disco balls as she placed the cup on the coffee table.

"I got your text," she said. "I'm proud of you and I'm glad it went well." Dionne smiled as she joined her love on the sofa.

"It was as if nothing had changed," Dionne sighed as she rested her head on Adriana's shoulder.

"Maybe because nothing has changed," Adriana replied. "She's still your sister."

"And Camryn is your sister."

"Camryn and I have other problems though," Adriana said. "Kamila obviously loves you no matter what. That's why she's able to accept you no matter who you love."

"I'd like to think my mom loves me too," Dionne muttered.

"She does." Adriana embraced her, giving her shoulder a comforting rub. "Valerie comes from a different time for one. Plus she's deeply involved in the church. It's a part of her, just like music is a part of you."

"How are you always so understanding?" Dionne asked. "Especially after all your family has done to you."

"It's not my entire family for one. I'm loved. Honestly, I believe somewhere deep inside, my mom and sister still love me too. But like I said, there are other issues in my family. I believe Camryn and I would always have some form of sibling rivalry even if I was straight. She and I have different fathers and you know how single mothers can tend to favor one child over another depending on how she feels about the father. My mom and my father don't exactly get along and she's still with Camryn's father who doesn't exactly care for me either. My sexuality was just another nail in the coffin as far as they're concerned. But I still love them. I can't carry that sort of resentment."

Dionne sat up and leaned in for a kiss. Adriana's lips were moist and soft as they parted, welcoming her. Adriana leaned backward, staring into Dionne's eyes.

"What was that for?" she asked.

"Your mind," Dionne smiled. "You're just so dope. I love the way you think."

"I'm glad. I wouldn't want to think you were just using me for my body."

"Well, your body is a definite perk," Dionne grinned as she leaned forward towards her. Adriana held out a hand, pressing Dionne gently on her breasts to hold her back.

"Slow down, potna," Adriana said. "Now that your sister finally knows about me, when do I get to meet her?"

"You want to talk about that now?" Dionne straightened herself as nervousness began to overtake her body. She was happy the cat was finally out of the bag. Kamila knew she was a lesbian and even knew she had a girlfriend. But she hadn't brought Adriana around anyone of importance besides her mother and that encounter wasn't exactly pretty. She knew she shouldn't expect Kamila to react the same as Valerie, but she couldn't help but worry.

"If not now, when?" Adriana asked, giving her back a gentle rub. "We plan on being together and she's a big part of your life. I don't want to keep having to tiptoe around whenever she comes over."

"You don't have to tiptoe," Dionne said. "She knows I have a girlfriend."

"But she doesn't know who I am. She's important to you. I'd like to think I am too."

"You are!" Dionne exclaimed, grabbing Adriana's hand to kiss her fingertips. "You're very important to me."

"Well then, it's time for me to meet your sister."

"Okay," Dionne relented. "I'll plan a dinner and invite her over. That way, you can meet Demarcus."

"So they're official now?"

"Yes indeed. I knew all along it would happen."

"That means she's finally done with Jesse?"

"I hope so," Dionne responded. "Only time will tell because it was hard for her to let that go."

Dionne put on some music and rested her head on Adriana's shoulder, catching her up on the events that took place earlier in the day.

Chapter Twenty-Four

Since I was no longer with Jesse and back living with Momma, I knew I'd need to find better-paying work soon. Before I did that, I had to take care of a few things. To start, I asked Demarcus to ride with me downstate to the prison to visit Jermaine. I thought about what Momma said to me. Losing Silas left me without my father figure but my actual birth father was still living and I didn't know much about him aside from the things Dionne would tell me.

As I waited for Demarcus in my car, I noticed Janette walking down the street. She twirled her burgundy weave around her fingers as her hips swung back and forth like a slinky. I sank in my seat, hoping she wouldn't notice me. I clearly failed because she walked directly to the car and tapped on my driver's side window.

MONIQUE SHANTAY

"What, Janette?" I asked as I rolled down the window.

"I see you're getting really bold, sitting parked outside Denise's house," she smirked.

"Why exactly do my actions concern you so much?"

"No reason. I mean, I'm just saying that a woman who's supposed to have a man she lives with shouldn't be spending so much time with her ex."

"And what exactly would you know about what a woman should be doing? I mean you've been on your back so much, I thought you were a mattress."

"I'm just saying," she said. "You and your girl Dionne act like y'all so much better than me. Y'all walk around with your noses in the air and treat me like I'm beneath you."

"When have I ever done that?" I asked. "I've never judged you without you giving me a reason."

"I remember how y'all would look at me when we were growing up. Y'all would judge me because I didn't grow up like y'all. It wasn't my fault my momma had issues when I was a kid."

I rolled my eyes and sighed at the foolishness that was coming from her lips.

"Just stop the madness, Janette," I snapped. "Just stop it. I'm seriously over it."

237

"I'm just being real," she said.

"Really delusional," I replied. "You made up issues with us in your own head based on your own insecurities. If you recall, I tried to give you a chance and be a friend to you. I can't speak for Dionne but I did. You messed that up, not me. You broke the girl code by messing with Demarcus when you knew we were together."

"So why can you forgive Demarcus and not me?"

"I can forgive Demarcus because he's actually remorseful for what he did. You feel I owe you something. You apparently feel the world owes you something. Nobody is hating on you, Janette. I honestly don't have time to spend my life hating on another black woman. We have enough of that in this world from everybody else. And you can miss me with blaming your momma for how you are because I was good to you and my momma is an alcoholic."

Janette stood and stared at me. It was if the wind was knocked from her sail as she mounted without a word. She put her hand on her hip and went back to twirling her hair.

"I'm done walking on eggshells around you, Janette. We're not friends. We haven't been friends for a very long time and it's not because I feel I'm better than you and it's not because I'm hating on you. It's because you're stuck in high school while I'm trying to master right now."

Demarcus came out of the house looking good in his black jeans and navy polo. He picked his chestnut curls as he walked toward the driver's side door and paused at the sight of Janette. He released an exasperated breath and changed direction, walking to the passenger side door.

"Hey Demarcus," Janette smiled.

"Don't talk to me like I fuck with you," Demarcus snapped.

"Damn, it's like that?"

"I haven't fucked with you since I found out about those pictures. You know that." Janette's eyes widened as Demarcus got into the passenger seat. She leaned down to my window and looked inside the car.

"You sure y'all should be riding around in a car together?" she asked.

"You think so, baby?" Demarcus asked, pulling my face towards him and giving me a passionate kiss. I turned back to Janette.

"Did you get that picture?" I asked.

"Forget y'all," she said, waving a hand and stomping off.

"Did you want to drive?" I asked.

"It's up to you," he said.

"I can start for now."

We got on the road for the six-hour drive to the prison. I played some old school Anita Baker and sang along as Demarcus scrolled down on his phone.

"That girl is a hot mess," I said.

"Who?"

"Janette."

"Are you okay?" he asked.

"About what?"

"I know you've had a lot of bad blood towards me and her for what happened."

"I'm over that, Demarcus. Since you've been back in my life, I understand you didn't do that to hurt me. Hell, I don't even think Janette meant to hurt me now that I think of it. Listening to her used to boil my blood but when she spoke today, I couldn't be mad at her. I actually hurt for her."

"Hurt for her?"

"Yeah. What she did to me may have been meant to hurt me when she did it. I mean it did hurt me for a long time but now I realize Janette's been searching for something her entire life. I hope she finds it one day but I can forgive her. I've already forgiven you."

"That's really big of you, babe," Demarcus said, rubbing my arm.

"I didn't do it for y'all," I smiled.

"I'd like to think you did it for me," Demarcus laughed.

"Well, I did do it for you in a way, but I did it for me too. This doesn't mean I'm going to have Janette over for a spades game or anything but I don't need to go through life feeling the need to punch her in the face either."

"I guess I can take that as long as you and I are okay," Demarcus smiled.

"Oh baby, we're fine," I replied. "I don't know if it's the newness of our relationship but you've just been amazing through everything I've been going through."

"We're not exactly new," Demarcus said.

"We're like new. We were kids when we dated before. Then we stopped talking and you went to Florida and I got with Jesse."

"Yeah, you gave that clown my loving."

"The point is, we're like new people," I laughed. "I'm looking forward to getting to know you in new ways."

"Me too, babe."

***

We arrived at the prison and went through security. It was my second time there and it was still difficult for me to see pregnant mothers and women with their children sitting in the waiting area to see prisoners. I thought of Dionne as a child, sitting with her mother as she waited to see Jermaine. As difficult as it was to see children in such a horrid place, had I known as a child that my father was alive and well, I'd probably want to sit in this room with my momma to see him. A little boy met eyes with me as he held hands with his mother. I smiled and waved at him. He flashed his dimples as he waved back.

"Do you ever think about having children?" Demarcus asked.

"Of course," I smiled. "Once my life isn't in shambles."

"Your life isn't in shambles, Kamila," he laughed.

"Okay maybe not in shambles, but I'd like to wait until things are more settled."

"I think you and I would make pretty babies," he whispered.

"I guess we'll have to wait and see."

One guard guided us to the window while two other guards walked with Jermaine on the other side. I picked up one phone while he picked up the other.

"I'm glad you decided to come back and see me," Jermaine smiled.

"I feel like I owed it to you - and to myself," I responded.

"You don't owe me anything."

"You've been in here all my life largely because of me."

"It's not your fault," Jermaine said.

"It's not that I'm blaming myself. I'm saying that your relationship with my mom and everything surrounding it, including my birth, put you in here. Had it not been for Dionne asking for a ride, I would have never gotten the chance to get to know you."

"It's not your fault," Jermaine said again.

"It's not about fault," I said. "I've spent too much time looking for blame. I'm not here for that. Admittedly, it's been difficult learning the truth and I haven't had much time to process that truth. However, I'd like to get to know you."

"I'd like that," Jermaine smiled. "By the way, I heard about Silas. I'm sorry for your loss."

"Thank you," I said. "It's been a pretty rough time."

"I'm sure." Jermaine's eyes shifted to Demarcus as he sat beside me.

"Excuse my manners," I said. "This is my boyfriend, Demarcus."

"Boyfriend?" he said. "Well, I guess I haven't been in your life long enough to put this cat to the test. Is he treating you right?"

"He's amazing," I grinned. "Considering the person I was with before, I could really do a lot worse." Demarcus smiled and nodded in agreement.

"As long as you're happy," Jermaine said. "I really appreciate you visiting me."

"I'll definitely be back," I replied. "And I'll be writing you too. I need all the family I can get."

"Well, you have your sister," Jermaine said.

"I've always had my sister."

"Visiting hours are up," a guard said, walking towards Jermaine.

"All right, man," he responded. "Just let me say goodbye to my daughter." His daughter. It felt incredible to hear him say those words.

"Until next time, baby girl," he smiled, placing his hand on the glass. I placed mine on the glass as well, meeting his hand.

"Until next time – Dad."

***

"So how do you feel?" Demarcus asked as he sat in the driver's seat to drive back home.

"I feel on top of the world," I sighed. "I have a dad I can talk to - who can actually talk back to me. A part of me feels like I'm betraying Royal by building a relationship with Jermaine. I've always known Royal as my dad."

"Maybe you can have two dads."

"Maybe so," I responded. "I'm still going to visit Royal. I've done it all my life and I still feel connected to him. It's weird because I never actually knew him."

"It doesn't matter if it's weird as long as it works for you."

I let back the passenger seat so I could get some rest on the ride home. Jay Z's *Money, Cash, Hoes* was interrupted as a call came through the speakers.

"Yo!" I said.

"Bitch, where you at?" Dionne asked.

"On my way back into town," I responded.

"From where?"

"My business!" I figured Dionne would be pissed if she knew I went to see Jermaine without her but this was something I needed to do. She had a lifetime of visits with him. I needed time to get to know him as my father.

"Well anyway, what y'all doing tomorrow night?" Dionne asked.

"Fucking," Demarcus interjected. I laughed.

"Ew," Dionne responded. "Well, y'all think y'all can close your legs long enough to come to my house for dinner? I want y'all to meet my girlfriend."

"Whaaaat?" I sang. "My sister kissing and telling now?"

"I've been with her for a while. I think it's getting serious so I figured it was time for her to meet my sister and her nasty ass boyfriend."

246

"You know I'm always down to meet family," Demarcus replied.

"Cool beans," I said. "Sounds like a date."

"Cool," Dionne exclaimed. "Maybe we can talk some business while I'm here. She works in the industry and she's going to help me get producing work. You know I had to tell her about my songwriter sister."

"Seriously?" I shrieked. "That would be dope! That's what I've always wanted to do."

"Okay, I'll see you tomorrow."

"Bet!"

Chapter Twenty-Five

Momma asked me to go with her to meet with the funeral director. We couldn't afford live doves or anything, but thanks to Jesse's I'm-Sorry-I-Beat-Your-Ass gift, I was able to sell the Bulgari watch in order to pay for a pretty decent funeral for Silas, as well as a burial next to Big Momma at Burr Oak Cemetery.

"His favorite color was blue," Momma explained through her shaky voice. "I want him in his best blue suit. And I want the flowers to be blue. I want everything to be blue. I know that's what he would want."

"Yes ma'am," the director replied. "We're getting him ready as we speak. Everything is set to go for tomorrow morning at 11."

"That will be great," I said. Momma was a wreck. She had been trying her best not to drink and we were working to repair our relationship, but Momma was spoiled. She had never had to take the reins on something major like this. When Big Momma died, Silas and I handled all the arrangements because Momma was too sauced to be of any help. At either rate, she was here, and I was proud of her efforts.

After we finished finalizing the arrangements, I took Momma to the mall to buy an outfit for the funeral. I could no longer afford Magnificent Mile shopping trips like the one I took with Dionne. We were back to shopping at Rainbow, but it didn't really matter to me as long as we looked cute. Big Momma always taught us to dress as if people were watching.

We walked into the store and I went over to the Misses section to help Momma pick an outfit. As much as I loved my mother, left to her own devices, she would have chosen something way too tight and far too young. I was not checking to receive the stares I used to get back when the playground kids would tell me about Momma's escapades.

She picked out a beautiful royal blue wrap dress that hugged her frame and a pair of strappy blue heels. She also decided to get a black sun hat with glasses ala Lynn Whitfield in *Madea's Family Reunion*. I was impressed by the outfit choice.

We stopped for a bite to eat in the food court. Momma got a Big Mac meal from McDonald's while I grabbed a rotisserie chicken sub from Subway.

"I really need to thank you for your help," Momma said.

"He's family," I responded. "Besides, I guess I should thank Jesse. It was the watch he gave me that paid for the funeral."

"What will you do now that you're not with him anymore?" Momma asked.

"Survive. I ate before I was with him and I'll continue to eat now that he's out of my life. Demarcus is no lawyer, but he makes decent money. I'm looking for better-paying work, plus Dionne thinks we may finally make a break in this music thing."

"Y'all never gave up on that stuff," Momma said. "No matter how much hell I gave you, you stuck to what you wanted to do."

"You know us Winter women are headstrong," I laughed.

"We are. But that drive didn't come from me. No, that's an Eason trait right there."

"You know, that's the first thing you've ever really told me about him," I said.

"Oh yes. Way back when, Jermaine was part of a singing group. He had a nice little following, too. That's part of what attracted me to him. That man could sing me out of my panties."

"TMI, Momma," I laughed as I covered my eyes.

"Girl, you're acting like I actually took my panties off. You know I had sex. You're sitting here, aren't you?"

"So my daddy was a singer?" I asked.

"Singer, songwriter, poet - that man had a way with words. That's where you get it from. You'd always carry those notebooks around with you and you had all the hope in the world. Sometimes it got on my nerves because after you were born, all I was ever told was my life was over because I was a mother. Plus I was carrying those dark secrets. I didn't have any hope and if I saw anyone who appeared to have hope around me, I thought they were tripping."

"You'd always tell me life was not a fairy tale," I said. "I did not want to believe you."

"No you didn't," she laughed. "You always had your head in the clouds."

"Well, in some ways, you were right. I've actually learned a lot from you recently."

"Like what?"

"I was so hard on you when I found out the truth, but I didn't think of how hard it was for you when all of that stuff happened. You carried all of those secrets and I'm sure you beat yourself up every step of the way. That's why you've had such a hard time with the alcohol. When Jesse cheated on me, you said that problems existed in life. You let me know that no relationship was perfect. Of course, things didn't work out with Jesse but I've learned from Demarcus that you can be flawed and still be in love."

"Yes you can," she said.

"I know you didn't care much for Demarcus when I was younger."

"I didn't like any boy you were dealing with as a child," she laughed. "Especially one who took your virginity. I didn't want to know you were having sex but I accepted the possibility."

"Demarcus never took my virginity," I laughed.

"He didn't?"

"No. That's why we broke up because I wasn't giving what Janette was selling!"

252

"Well hell, I guess I hated the boy for nothing!"

"I'm glad we're actually being mother and daughter and aren't at each other's throats," I said. "I wish Silas could see this."

"He can see it," Momma replied, looking towards the ceiling.

"I just wish I could have been there."

"I'm sorry for that," Momma said. "I could have made sure you knew. I was being petty because you weren't taking my calls."

"I was petty by not accepting your calls," I responded.

"Let's just say we were both wrong."

"I can agree to that."

We finished our dinner and walked through the parking lot to my car so I could drop Momma off at home. The humid Chicago heat hit my face as Momma rolled down the car windows.

"I can turn on the air," I said.

"Girl, save your gas," Momma replied.

"Momma, that outside air is nothing but the devil's armpits smacking us in the face. It's fine."

"You're not with Jesse no more," she said. "Save your coins."

Ignoring her, I turned on the air conditioner and rolled up the windows, turning on the child locks in case she wanted to protest.

That's fine," she shrugged. "It's your money."

I parked in front of the family building and helped Momma carry the bags up to her apartment

"So what do you have planned for the night?" Momma asked.

"Dionne invited Demarcus and me over to meet her special someone."

"You mean her girlfriend?"

"How did you know about that?" I asked.

"Girl, I think you were the last person on the planet to know. I used to catch Dionne kissing little girls around the neighborhood all the time."

"I wonder why she never told me."

"She didn't tell me," Momma replied. "I don't even think she knew I caught her."

"Well, why didn't you tell me?"

"It wasn't my place to say," Momma responded.

"I guess. Well, she's been seeing this person for a while and she wants me to meet her."

"I'm happy you've always had her in your life," Momma said.

"Me too," I replied.

Chapter Twenty-Six

After spending quality time with Momma, I walked down the street to meet Demarcus at his place so he could drive to Dionne's. I changed into a white sundress for Dionne's dinner but had to pair it with my baby pink sweater as the air had become a bit cool at sundown. I rang the doorbell and sat on the steps so Demarcus would know I was waiting outside. My cell phone buzzed, notifying me of a text.

Jesse: How are you? Can we talk?

Knots formed in my stomach as I quickly deleted the text from my phone. I didn't care to know why he was contacting me and also didn't want to upset Demarcus by bringing Jesse back into my life.

Demarcus walked down the steps wearing a black polo and khaki shorts. He picked his curls and smiled at me as I stood from my seat on the steps.

"Hey baby," he said, wrapping his arm around my waist and kissing my cheek.

"Hey yourself," I smiled. I stared into the sparkles in his eyes as they melted every ounce of tension that text message left in my stomach. "I'm happy to see you."

"You know I'm always happy to see you," he responded. "Ready to go?"

"Sure am!" I turned to walk down the steps.

"Whoa," Demarcus called from behind me. I turned to look at him as a tinge of panic fluttered inside my chest.

"What?"

"I like," he said, waving his finger up and down at me.

"Like what?"

"That dress. You're showing your legs. I know you don't do that often." I beamed at him. He noticed my effort. He wasn't around for my accident nor was he around during the years my confidence wavered due to my scars as Jesse was, but he paid attention to me. This only made me love him more.

"I'm making steps," I replied.

"I'm impressed."

Demarcus opened the passenger side door to his Crown Victoria and I stepped inside. He walked around to the other side of the car, got in driver's side and we made the 20 minute trip to Dionne's place. The sun had taken its bow for the day and the moon was full and bright as we arrived to Dionne's apartment and walked up the steps. I could smell delicious aromas as we approached Dionne's door.

"Something smells good," Demarcus said.

"It sure does," I added. I was still full from having lunch with Momma but I was not opposed to making a to-go plate to take home. I knocked on the door.

"Open the door, bitch!" I shouted.

"Why you gotta call the girl a bitch in front of her woman?" Demarcus asked.

"Baby, if she's going to be with my sister, she may as well get used to how we talk to each other. Besides, if she and Dionne are as serious as she says, I'm pretty sure she's used to a few swear words. I mean, this is Dionne."

"You're right," Demarcus laughed.

The door flung open as Dionne stood on the other side, serving full Erykah Badu headwrap realness. I was surprised to see she opted to wear a lavender knee-length A-line skirt which was a bit different from the floor length skirts she would normally wear. She even wore heels.

"Bitch, who are you and what are you doing in my sister's crib?" I laughed.

"Hoe, you know it's me," Dionne retorted. "My baby likes my legs."

"Your baby? Let me get in there and meet this baby!" Demarcus followed me into the apartment. On the sofa sat a tall, slender woman with chocolate brown skin. Half of her ebony locs were pulled back into a messy bun while the rest hung to her shoulders. She wore black slacks and a black top with spaghetti straps as she sat on the couch with her legs crossed, reading a book.

Dionne pushed past Demarcus and me and walked over to her baby's side.

"Kamila, Demarcus, this is my baby Adriana. Adriana, this is my sister, Kamila, and her boyfriend, Demarcus." Adriana placed the book aside and stood from the couch, reaching to shake Demarcus's hand.

"Demarcus, a pleasure," she smiled. She stepped towards me and embraced me in a huge hug.

"Kamila! Dionne talks about you all the time."

"I wish I could say the same," I responded. "But it's nice to meet you."

Demarcus and I took a seat on the loveseat as Adriana sat back on the couch. Dionne rushed back to the kitchen to check on dinner.

"So what are you reading?" I asked.

"Ten Hours to Mexico," she responded.

"I've never heard of that one. Who wrote it?"

"Junior Love. He's is an amazing poet who writes from a unique LGBT perspective. Plus he's an independent artist and we could always use more black writers."

"I think I like you already," I laughed.

"I hope so," she replied.

"So Adriana," Demarcus said. "Where are you from?"

"I'm from Lombard."

"Oh, a suburban kid," I said. I silently hoped my sister didn't go out and get a female version of Jesse, seeing as he was also born and raised in the suburbs.

"Yes, kind of," Adriana said. "I grew up in Ida B Wells but my dad started a music company with his brother and we made enough to move out of the projects before gentrification got a hold of them."

"I know what you mean. Dionne and I both grew up in Cabrini Green."

"I know," Adriana replied.

"My Big Momma was evicted when I was in elementary school. They made up some bullshit reason to do it but it was probably for the best. Not too long after we moved, the building we lived in was demolished. Things haven't been the same since."

"I'm sure," Adriana said.

"They call it community development," Demarcus added. "But how does building expensive ass high rises add to the community? They aren't doing it for the people who live there."

"Of course not," Adriana said. "See, I like y'all."

"I think I like you too," I smiled.

"I ain't fixing no plates," Dionne called as she emerged from the kitchen. She carried one plate in each hand, filled with spinach pasta. She walked over to the couch where Adriana sat, placing a plate in front of her love.

"You're a rude little witch," I smirked.

"We were talking about gentrification," Adriana said, kissing Dionne on her cheek.

"Crooked motherfuckers," Dionne murmured.

"See?" I whispered to Demarcus. "I'll go fix our plates." I got up from the couch and walked into Dionne's kitchen. I pulled two white glass plates with gold trim from a brown cabinet, pulled two forks from the silverware drawer and filled the plates with fettuccini pasta and Spinach Alfredo sauce. Balancing one plate in each hand, I joined the others in the living room. Demarcus stood to greet me, taking one of the plates from my hand.

"Thank you, baby," he smiled. "Adriana was telling us how she's working with her father at his record label."

"It's something like a family business," Adriana explained.

"Oh yes," I smiled as I sat back on the couch. "Dionne was telling me about that."

"She tells me you're a songwriter."

"Something like that," I replied. "I write as a hobby and for Dionne and me but I've never written for anyone else."

"Do you have some of your work with you?"

"I always have work with me," I grinned. I put my fork on the plate and placed it on the table. Getting my purse from the living room closet, I pulled out my notebook and gave it to Adriana.

"Do you mind?" she asked.

"Please. It's all song lyrics along with some ideas for songs." I sat back next to Demarcus as Adriana thumbed through the notebook pages. She skimmed through some of the pages while taking longer looks at others.

"Did you write the songs you recorded with Dionne?" she asked.

"Most of them," I responded. "Dionne contributed on a few of them."

"This is really good stuff," Adriana said. "We have some artists who are really good singers but they're not the best writers. You could make good money as a songwriter."

"I've heard things about it but I just never knew how to break in the songwriting business."

"I'm sure my dad and uncle can help you out with that," she replied. "We're mostly a local company although we're looking to expand to Atlanta."

"That's hot," Demarcus said. "I used to stay not too far from there."

"Oh yeah?" Adriana asked. "Where about?"

"My pops lives in St. Petersburg."

"Is that where you're from?"

"No, I'm from here. Moms sent me to live with my pops after I got into some trouble in these streets. I came back when she got sick."

"I'm sorry to hear that. Is she okay now?" Adriana asked.

"She's in assisted living right now. I came back to take care of her but I got blessed in the process." Demarcus gave my hand a gentle rub as he smiled at me.

"That's so sweet," Adriana smiled.

"So how long have you two been together?" I asked. Dionne's face became flushed as she took a hard sip of her lemon water. She looked to Adriana as I caught a rare glimpse of my sister being genuinely speechless.

"We've been friends for about a year but we started dating seriously about seven months ago," Adriana said. I watched my sister as she flashed a nervous smile at her girlfriend.

"Dee," I said. "I don't think I've ever seen your face so red. You're so cute!" Dionne released an uncomfortable laugh.

"She's been so afraid of telling you about us," Adriana said.

"Why?" I asked. "We talk about everything, or at least I thought we did." Dionne looked down at her lap and fumbled her fingers.

"This has always been such a private part of my life," she said. "I tried to tell my mom when I was younger and she told me I was going to hell. She even had the pastor come to the house to pray the gay away. Even now, she calls Adriana a phase and says she prays for the day I grow out of it."

"That's terrible," I said.

"I know Ms. Mary kept you in the church and raised you kind of old school so I wasn't sure how you'd take it."

"Girl, you didn't give me the chance," I replied. I got up from the loveseat and squeezed between Dionne and the arm of the couch, wrapping my arm around her.

"You're my sister," I said. "You were my sister even when I didn't know you were my sister. I love you regardless of who you choose to love as long as you're happy. I mean, I don't know about dealing with suburban people for my own reasons, but Adriana seems like a cool chick."

Dionne took a sigh of relief and wrapped her arms around my neck.

"You don't know how much better this makes me feel," she said.

"I got your back," I responded.

We spent the remainder of the evening discussing politics, music, and love. It was amazing to simply be a girl in love and not only that, be with Dionne while she openly showed love to someone she cared about. This was a different side of Dionne. She was softer, sweeter, and more affectionate. Adriana brought out the softer side of my usually rough-around-the-edges sister while I was able to simply relax with Demarcus without having to obsess over putting on a good impression.

"We probably shouldn't stay much later," I said, looking at the time on my cell phone. It was approaching 11 pm and Silas's funeral was early the next morning.

"Yeah, we probably should be getting to bed soon too," Dionne responded. "You know I gotta come through and show support."

"I appreciate it." Dionne and I hugged as Adriana stood from the couch behind her.

"I heard about your uncle," she said as she stepped forward to hug me. "My condolences to you and your family."

"Thank you. It was so good meeting you. Make sure you take care of my sister."

"I can walk you guys out," Dionne said.

"Girl, it's late," Demarcus responded. "You guys rest. We got this."

After saying goodbye and grabbing our things, Demarcus and I walked down the stairs and outside to the car. As the breezy night air sent chills down my legs, I was relieved that I opted to bring my sweater.

"What did you think of Adriana?" I asked as we got into the car to head home.

"She seems like a cool chick," he responded. "She definitely has a brain in her head which is pretty rare these days."

"I don't know much about Dionne's love life," I laughed. "But I know she doesn't care for idiots."

"Neither do you, except for that last clown." As Demarcus laughed, I could feel the knots resurfacing in my stomach. He studied my expression as a look of concern formed on his face.

"You gonna tell me?" he asked. My breaths began to shorten as a tight sensation formed in my chest.

"I got a message earlier today," I said. "I deleted it. I wasn't going to tell you about it. I was just going to act like it didn't exist."

"What did he have to say?"

"He says he wants to talk."

"You don't have shit to say to him," Demarcus snapped. I felt nauseous as his voice rose in anger.

"I know," I replied.

"I'm sorry," he said. "Don't get upset. I just don't want him to hurt you again."

"I have no intentions of speaking to him. I just didn't want you to be upset."

"I would have been upset if you were talking to him and I didn't know about it," he answered. "I'm not upset with you because he contacted you." My body shook with nervousness as I responded with a quiet nod. Demarcus pulled the car to the side of the road. He lifted my chin, directing me to look into his eyes.

"No," he said. "I don't want you afraid of me. I'm not him. There will be times when I get upset with you or we'll disagree, but I don't ever want you to be afraid of me. You have never been that girl. Don't start now."

"Okay," I responded. It's going to take time for me to work through this fear."

"I understand. Moms went through this with my pops when I was a kid. I used to watch her cry when Pops would do her wrong. I told myself as a shorty I would never make a woman cry the way she did and I can't respect these fuck boys that are out here putting their hands on women."

His eyes were wide and filled with care and concern for me. I felt his love radiate throughout my entire being as all the anxiety I felt began to melt away.

"We should probably get home," I said. "We have a full day ahead of us."

"Yeah, we should," Demarcus said. He pulled back on the road to drop me off at home.

Chapter Twenty-Seven

The sky was colored a faint shade of gray as morning arrived. I hadn't slept much the night before as grief and dread plagued my weary stomach. This was the day we were gathering to say goodbye to the man who helped raise me from the day I was born. Although I knew this life was only temporary, he was one person I foolishly thought would always be around. I wasn't ready to say goodbye to him. I wanted one more phone call. One more lecture about being the bigger person. One more day.

I dragged my lethargic body from the comfort of my bed and shuffled into the bathroom for a shower. Before going to bed the night before, I had hung a pale blue lace dress with matching shawl on the back of the bathroom door. The warm water from the shower massaged my skin as I lathered myself with passion fruit shower gel. As I began to rinse myself, I could hear a knock on the bathroom door.

"Mila," Momma called. "I'm making breakfast if you want some."

"I'll be up there," I responded. I finished rinsing myself and stepped out of the shower, drying off with one of Big Momma's fluffy towels.

After getting dressed, I walked up the steps to Momma's apartment. The sound of Chicago House music shook the walls as Momma stood over the stove, cooking pancakes and eggs, and bacon. She didn't have the magic touch Silas had with making breakfast, but her cooking wasn't so bad when she did cook for me. I walked to the refrigerator and poured myself a glass of orange juice as I waited for her to finish.

"Thanks for breakfast," I said. "I don't have much of an appetite."

"You feeling okay?"

"My stomach has been bothering me a lot," I replied. "I think it's all the stress that's been going on."

"Are you sure that's all it is?" Momma asked, placing a plate of food in front of me.

"I'm pretty sure," I replied. "It's been a rough time from everything with Jesse and Demarcus to losing Silas, plus finding out about Jermaine. I think I just need some rest."

"Maybe so," Momma responded, taking a bite of her eggs. I looked down at the plate as my stomach did flip-flops. Normally, I would love the smell of bacon but right then, all I wanted to do was…

I jumped up from the table and ran to Momma's bathroom, spewing my troubles into the toilet. My face moistened with sweat as my stomach evicted Dionne's dinner from my body. Momma stood in the bathroom doorway shaking her head as I looked up from the toilet.

"That ain't no stress," she said. "Looks like you might wanna go to the drug store."

"I'm not pregnant," I protested. "I'm just not ready to say goodbye to Silas."

Momma shook her head again and walked back to the kitchen. I stood up from the toilet and leaned over the sink to rinse the taste of vomit from my mouth. I had just ended things with Jesse and was just starting with Demarcus. I was underemployed and living in my grandmother's house. I was not ready to have a child.

"I'm gonna go back downstairs," I said to Momma as I emerged from the bathroom.

"Go get you some saltines and a pregnancy test from Walgreens," she commanded from the kitchen table. "That ain't no stress."

I ignored her and walked back downstairs. Trying my best to push Momma's words from my mind, I laid back in bed to rest for a while as my stomach was continuing to churn. I reached over to the nightstand to check my phone. There was one text from Dionne.

Dionne: Thank you guys for coming out last night and thank you for your words. I'm not sure if I say this enough, but I'm so happy to have you as my real life sister. I feel so much better now.

I replied to her text.

Me: I guess that's what blood sisters are for.

As I went back to my message menu, I noticed another new text message.

Jesse: After all we've been through, I can't believe you would just throw us away like this for some street bum. You at least owe me some sort of conversation or closure.

The pain in my stomach suddenly increased as anxiety flooded my body.

"Not today, Jesse," I said to myself as I placed the phone face down on the nightstand. My eyelids grew heavy as I drifted off to sleep.

***

I felt a tap on my feet, waking me from my nap. I opened my eyes to see Demarcus standing at the foot of the bed, wearing a navy blue suit with a pale blue tie.

"Wake up, sleepyhead," he smiled. I sat up in bed as my head began to throb.

"Are you okay?" he asked.

"I feel kind of sick," I responded. "I think its stress."

"You have been going through a lot," Demarcus replied. He sat beside me on the bed, rubbing his fingers through my hair.

"Momma thinks I'm pregnant," I laughed.

"Do you think so?"

"I can't be pregnant."

"Is it you don't want to be pregnant or you don't think you're pregnant?" I sat in silence as I pondered his question.

"Kamila?"

"I think its stress, Demarcus. I'm here at my grandma's house and I'm underemployed. Plus we just got together and I'm trying to take things slow."

"You're worrying too much," he said, kissing my forehead. "I make good money plus you and Dee are doing your thing with this music. There's no telling what connections Adriana could get you. And I'm here for you, Mila. I may not have that Bennett money but I can make sure we're all okay if you let me." I looked into his eyes and smiled at the man who was already working out a situation based on a possibility. I didn't know if I was pregnant. It really could have just been stress.

"How would you feel if I was pregnant?" I asked.

"Are you kidding me?" he smiled. "I used to dream about making you Mrs. Cruz. I thought I lost that dream forever until you came back into my life."

"Well, there's something else," The guilt stabbed at my inner being as I stared downward at my lap.

"What?"

"Jesse," I responded. "We hooked up while I was with him. If I am pregnant, what if the baby is his?"

"Don't worry about that," Demarcus hugged me tight. "We'll be okay either way. He's not going to hurt you again.

Not while I'm around." I collapsed into his chest as tears streamed from my eyes. He cupped my chin with his hand and lifted my eyes so they would meet his.

"Hey," he said. "None of that. You don't even know if you're pregnant and you're worrying like this."

"I never wanted this to be my life," I sobbed. "I used to talk about girls like this."

"You were young and didn't know any better. It takes living life for you to see just how crazy it can be. Shit, back in the day, I said I'd be sitting somewhere like Diddy with my own conglomeration or some shit. I didn't see myself as a factory worker. You never know where life can take you and you can't judge yourself for your journey or anyone else for theirs."

"I'm sure others will judge," I sighed.

"If there's something to judge, I'm sure they have their skeletons too. Fuck 'em!" I cracked a fragile smile as he pulled me back into a hug.

"That's my girl," he said.

"Kamila," Momma called from the stairway. "The limo's here!"

As I leaned forward to kiss Demarcus, he held up a hand in protest.

"You just woke up and you may have been throwing up," he said.

"You want me to be Mrs. Cruz and you can't handle a little bit of vomit residue?" I laughed.

"You're fucking right!" I slapped his shoulder as I got up from the bed. I went to the bathroom to freshen up so we could leave.

I stood frozen as I read the sign posted by the door. *Homegoing Celebration for Silas T. Winter.* Those words just didn't go together for me. In my mind, I hoped I would wake up and someone would tell me it was a dream or some cruel joke. I walked into the room and stood towards the back of it, getting a distant glimpse at the casket that lay towards the front of the room. I wasn't ready to see him in that way just yet, but Momma insisted I go with her as she didn't want to be alone. We held hands and walked together down the aisle to the front of the room where Silas laid in his casket. The man inside wore a blue suit that I recognized, but his face did not look like the face of the man that had been in my life since birth. I stood in silence, searching within my mind for words to make sense of my feelings. My body felt numb as I watched my uncle laying in the last place I would see his face.

As I turned to find a seat, well-wishers began to fill the room. There were distant family members I hadn't seen since Big Momma's funeral seven years earlier, and friends of Silas's from the projects who I hadn't seen since I was in preschool. People hugged and exchanged stories of the good old days before the funeral service began and we all took our seats.

"Good afternoon, brothers and sisters," the pastor said as he stepped to the podium.

"Good afternoon," everyone replied.

"We are gathered here to celebrate the life of Brother Silas T. Winter. But I'm here to tell you that although you may feel sad today, Silas is somewhere smiling. He would not want to come back from where he is even if he could because he's with God now. He isn't feeling any more pain or sadness. And at some point in time, we will all get to go join Brother Silas and sit with the Father in a place of glory." Hand claps and shouts echoed throughout the crowd as the pastor delivered words of encouragement and praise.

"I'm now going to open the floor to those who'd like to come up and say a few words about Brother Silas," the pastor said.

Momma, Dionne, Silas's friend Kevin, his daughter Keisha, and I all got in line to speak. Momma stepped to the podium, wiping tears from her eyes as she looked down at her big brother.

"It's hard to get up here and talk about my brother like this," she said. "Our dad passed away when I was a year old so, throughout my childhood, it was Momma, Silas and me. He was always there ready to knock out any boy who wanted to try me. He taught me how to fight and in many ways, he taught me how to love. So many times I felt like I let him down. He used to tell me I could go to college and accomplish anything in life, but he never judged me when my baby Kamila was born. He just stepped up and took on the role as father. He was there for her in times I couldn't be and I'll forever love him for that. It was hard when I lost my momma and now my brother's gone. I don't know how I'm going to hold on but as long as I have my baby with me, I'll do my best. Thank you." Weighted tears fell from my eyes at Momma's words. She didn't often express feelings like this to me as a child. There were many times I felt as if she didn't care at all so it felt good to hear what she had to say.

Momma returned to her seat in the front pew as Dionne stepped up to the podium.

"Many of y'all know me. My name is Dionne Eason. I'm Kamila's best friend - and sister - and Silas was like a father to me. My dad has been in prison all my life and many of the kids around the hood didn't have their fathers around either. Silas was the type of man who'd teach boys how to be men and he'd teach girls what type of men to be around. Any of you younger ones in here know if Silas caught you doing some foolishness, he'd beat your tail and go tell your momma he did it. Sometimes, I'd be so mad at him, but he made me a better woman for it. I wanna give my condolences to Sheila and Kamila. Silas, we're all going to miss you. Thank you." Dionne stepped down from the podium and held me in a tight hug as Kevin stepped up to speak.

"I love you," she whispered.

"I love you back," I said.

"My name is Kevin Harper. I've known Silas since back in high school when we played together on the football team. I remember when I first met him. All I could think was, 'I'm glad this dude is running beside me and not towards me.' Silas was a big dude. But we became instant friends. I used to stay at the house and Ms. Mary would cook up a storm. I remember the time she tore our tails up after she caught us sneaking girls into the house while she was at work. But what I'm going to miss the most about this brother is the phone calls. It didn't matter what time it was or what was going on. If you needed a listening ear, Silas was there. He was the one who would get you right together. I don't know who's going to be there to get me together now. I'm gonna miss you, brother." Kevin wiped away a tear as he stepped from the podium, giving me a hug.

"It's good to see you," he whispered.

"It's good to see you too," I replied. "Thank you."

"My name is Keisha Harper," Keisha said, stepping to the podium. "I'm the daughter of Kevin Harper, the man who just got done speaking. Silas was my godfather. He would always come get me and take me and Kamila to the park and to the movies. Kamila, Dionne and I would run around playing while he and my daddy would play spades or dominoes. My only regret was losing touch with him after I went away to college. I lost touch with a lot of people. At a time, Kamila and I were like sisters too. I miss that. I just want to say we all should make the best of the time we have with each other while we're all still here. I love you all. Thank you." Keisha stepped from the podium and the two of us hugged.

"I've missed you," she said.

"I've missed you too," I replied. "We'll do better."

Now it was on me. I was the last person in line to speak. I stepped up to the podium.

"Hi. Most of y'all know me. I'm Kamila Winter. Silas was my uncle. In many ways, he was more than that to me. There's so much I could say and it's hard for me to get everything out without breaking down in tears so I wrote and recorded something. Thank you to my sister Dionne for providing the music." I pulled out a tape recorder and put it to the microphone.

I got a lump in my throat

This can't be real life

I can't imagine

No longer looking into your eyes

I can't imagine

No longer receiving advice

I can't imagine

Silas not being in my life

I'm supposed to say goodbye

But I got tears in my eyes

No matter how I try

I just let the words apply

My Uncle Sy

This is crazy

I spent life as uncle's baby

You been gone for a short time

MONIQUE SHANTAY

But things been out of order lately

It's just me and my mom

I can't lean on your arm

Or watch the games

And it's insane

But you're no longer feeling pain

So I guess I find solace

In the fact you found peace

At either rate I thank you

Because without you there's no me

So I'll keep the things you taught me

I'll keep them in my heart

We'll be together again

And then we'll never again depart

Until then, I'll hold it down

And make sure all know your name

We'll all miss you, Uncle Silas

Things will never be the same

I placed the recorder back into my pocket and took my seat next to Momma as the pastor stood back at the podium. Two members of the funeral home staff approached the casket and removed the flowers from the top of it. They opened the casket and walked back to the side of the room as the knots that would often frequent the lining of my stomach showed their presence once again.

"Brothers and sisters," the pastor said. "Now it is time for a final view of the body as we depart. The burial will take place at Burr Oak Cemetery in Alsip, Illinois, followed by the repast at the Winter family home. May the Lord bless you all in the name of the Father, the Son, and the Holy Ghost. Go in peace."

Momma and I stood at the front of the line as we prepared ourselves to take our last view of Silas. Demarcus shuffled through the crowd to be by my side as my body began to feel numb. As I stared down into the casket at Silas's body, I was flushed with sadness, fear, and anger. I wanted him to get up from that casket and tell me this wasn't really happening. I was angry with him for leaving me without telling me goodbye. I was angry with myself for being so caught up in my own foolishness that I couldn't be there with him. My knees buckled underneath me as violent tears escaped my eyes. Demarcus wrapped his arm around me, pulling me up and guiding me out into the hallway.

"You're okay, baby," he said. "You're okay."

"I'm not," I cried. "I don't know if I'll ever be okay again."

Guests filled the hallway after saying their final goodbyes. Kevin along with a few other of Silas's childhood friends carried the casket from the room to the hertz as onlookers followed behind, filing to their cars.

"Are you going to be okay?" Demarcus asked. I nodded as I left him to join Momma in the limo.

The tail end of a storm dropped its last bit of rain as about twenty cars lined the streets, trailing each other to the cemetery. Some drivers who weren't part of the funeral party followed behind for a while so they could run red lights while others attempted to cut us off to get where they were trying to go. I sat in a corner of the limo, leaning against the window while holding my stomach. We arrived at Burr Oak as everyone parked in line. Kevin and the rest of the pallbearers carried Silas' casket to the empty plot next to Big Momma's grave. My heels sank into the soft wet soil as I walked through the grass to Silas's plot.

"And now we say goodbye to our brother Silas," the pastor said. "From dust, we all come and to dust we all return. Ashes to ashes, dust to dust." Silas's casket lowered into the ground as Momma and Kevin dropped handfuls of dirt on top.

"Do you want to do it, baby girl?" Kevin asked. I shook my head. I wanted no part of burying Silas. I didn't want him in that hole at all. As I turned to walk away, Kevin tapped my shoulder.

"You know, I've known you since you were a little girl," he said. "Silas always looked out for my Keisha and I know he'd want me to step up and look out for you."

"I appreciate that," I replied. "I like what Keisha had to say at the funeral. I think we all need to do better."

Momma walked up behind Kevin as tears streamed from her face. She tapped Kevin's shoulder and he turned to her.

"Hey sis," he smiled, embracing her.

"My brother's gone," she cried.

"I know, baby," he replied. "But we're still here for you."

"Thank you. You're sweet."

"I gotta get back to Keisha but I'll catch up with you ladies at the house," Kevin said.

Momma and I stood and looked at Silas's gravesite as everyone else began to head for their cars.

"We should probably get going, Momma," I said. "Everyone's probably on their way to the house."

"You're right," she responded.

"You know, Momma, Silas and Big Momma are gone now. They're not here to make us act like mother and daughter anymore. We're all we've got now."

"You're sort of right. You still need to go to Walgreens."

"I'm not pregnant, woman!" I laughed. We walked back to the limo.

Every hair on my body stood alert as the limo pulled up to the family building. Jesse's silver BMW sat parked in front. Momma looked at the car and back at me.

"Are you okay?" she asked. I nodded, but she knew I was lying. I pulled my cell phone from my purse and called Demarcus.

"Hello?"

"How far away are you?" I asked.

"I just stopped at the house to change out of this hot suit," Demarcus responded. "Why?"

287

"Jesse is in front of the house," I said as panic quickened my voice.

"The fuck? I'll be right down there!"

"Thank you," I whimpered.

Jesse stepped out of his car, wearing blue jeans, a white collared shirt, and sneakers. He walked with a smooth calmness to the limo and tapped on the window.

"Kamila," he called. "Are you in there? We need to talk."

"Jesse, it's my uncle's funeral," I responded. "Do you need to do this now?"

"You won't return my calls. I didn't know what else to do."

"How about leaving me alone?"

"I'm gonna go start on the food," Momma whispered, reaching for the door on the opposite side. She got out of the limo and nodded to Jesse as she walked briskly to the building. I locked both doors before Jesse could open either of them to enter the limo.

"Kamila, this is silly," he said. "We've been together too long for this. You know you still love me."

"I'm done, Jesse!" I shouted, curling over to hold my stomach. "I can't handle this right now."

"Kamila," he said as he jiggled the door handle. "Open the door. OPEN THE DOOR!" I leaned over and laid on the back seat as his anger continued to grow.

"You know, I came over here to do you a favor. You're not...." Jesse's voice was cut off by the sound of a loud thud. I recovered from my fetal position and looked out the window. Jesse laid on the sidewalk holding his jaw as Demarcus stood over him with his best Muhammad Ali stance.

"The lady asked you to leave her alone," Demarcus said.

"I could have you arrested," Jesse cried.

"Go ahead," Demarcus answered. "You're over here trespassing. The lady said she didn't want you here. Now I suggest you get on somewhere." Demarcus turned to see me watching from the window. He smiled and waved his hand to me, ushering for me to come out. As I stepped outside, Kevin walked towards the house with his brother.

"You're safe, baby," Demarcus said. "He's not going to bother you again. Ain't that right, Jesse?"

"Oh, we got a problem, Buster Brown?" Kevin asked as he approached us. Kevin was not a person Jesse wanted to tangle with. He was the type who would gladly go to prison if the cause was worth it.

"Nah," Demarcus said. "He was just leaving. Right?" Jesse nodded as he stood up from the sidewalk, dusting the debris from his clothing.

"I'll be leaving now," Jesse said. His initial cockiness disappeared as he stared fearfully at Kevin and his brother.

"This is my second time whooping your ass," Demarcus said. "Don't make me do it a third time. It's starting to become sad." Jesse smirked at Demarcus while nursing his jaw as he stumbled back towards his car. Demarcus wrapped me in a tight hug, letting me know I was safe as Jesse drove away.

"I like your style young man," Kevin smiled as he extended his hand to Demarcus. "I'm Kevin."

"Demarcus," he responded, shaking Kevin's hand.

"I appreciate the way you took care of baby girl here," Kevin replied. "You know, I grew up with Silas and helped raise this girl. I'm sure he'd only want the best for her."

"That's all I want," Demarcus shrugged.

"Then we're good," Kevin smiled, patting Demarcus on the back. The four of us joined the rest of the party that began to form in the backyard. I sat at one of the red picnic tables Momma and I had lined around the yard as guests lined up to fix plates of barbecue ribs, chicken, sausage links, and burgers as well as sides of collard greens, macaroni, sweet potatoes, cabbage, spaghetti, baked beans, and potato salad. We celebrated Silas all night that night. The tears began to dry as the cards and dominoes were pulled out. We played one of Silas's favorite songs; Outkast's *So Fresh and So Clean*. It had been years since seeing many of the attendants, and it would probably be years if ever when I'd see most of these people again, but we were enjoying each other. At that time, Momma and I were the last Winters standing, but we were surrounded by family and love. The mistakes she made didn't matter. The mistakes I made did not matter. It didn't matter if Royal was my daddy or Jermaine was my daddy because I had a sister in Dionne no matter what. If I was sick from pregnancy instead of stress, it would work out the way that God intended. I wasn't alone. I had Momma, Dionne, Demarcus, Keisha and Kevin and I knew Silas was still with me. I decided then if I was pregnant, and if the baby was a boy, his name would be Silas Trevon Cruz. He would have been conceived by imperfect means, just as I was, but it would all be part of God's perfect plan. We may make mistakes, but He never does.

Acknowledgments

First and foremost, I'd like to thank Patrick, the love of my life, for always supporting my creative endeavors. Without you, there would be no open-mic, no writing events, and no confidence to write this book.

To my wonderful children, thank you all for being my constant motivation and for being my comfort in this storm we call life.

To my siblings, Brandon, Dominique, and Vanessa, thank you all for being my ride or die support system.

To my mom, Cynthia, thank you for always encouraging me and keeping me calm when life makes me crazy.

To my friends, near and far, old and new, thank you all for contributing to a better me. Kandace, thank you for being a never-ending source of support. To my new friends, James and Ronny, thank you both for welcoming me into the fold and making me feel like a sister. I love you all!

A special thanks is in order to the Write Club of the Ouachita Parish Public Library. Jade, Kristy, Will, Nathan, Evangeline, Chris, Spencer, Ashley, and Eileen, thank you all for welcoming me, inviting me to participate in NaNoWriMo, and helping me see that I could write a book in the first place.

Lastly, I'd like to thank Ronny and Erica for taking the time to beta read my book. You guys are awesome!

If I have forgotten anyone at all, please charge it to my head and not my heart. Until next time!

    − Monique